THE AFTER
SCHOOL
DETECTIVE
CLUB

THE SECRET OF RAGNAR'S GOLD

The After-School Detective Club series:

The Case of the Smuggler's Curse

The Secret of Ragnar's Gold

The Mystery in the Marshes
(available from January 2023)

THE AFTER SCHOOL DETECTIVE CLUB

THE SECRET OF RAGNAR'S GOLD

Mark Dawson

WRITING WITH ALLAN BOROUGHS

ILLUSTRATED BY BEN MANTLE

WELBECK
FLAME

First published in 2022 by Welbeck Flame
An imprint of Welbeck Children's Limited,
part of Welbeck Publishing Group.
20 Mortimer Street, London W1T 3JW

ISBN: 978 1 80130 029 2

Printed and bound by CPI Group (UK)

10 9 8 7 6 5 4 3 2 1

To My Family

Lucy

Brave, loyal and athletic. She wants to be

an Olympian so don't get in her way . . .

Max

The geek with a wicked sense of humor.

Self-styled child genius – just don't tell his mom.

Joe

Adventurous, funny and a great cook – but

don't believe everything he says.

Charlie

Fierce as a lion, she loves her dog Sherlock more

than people. Don't ever call her Charlotte!

Sherlock

Loud bark, cold nose,

big heart – the fifth

member of the club.

THE CHURCH

THE LAKE

THE CASTLE

THE BURIAL MOUND

TUNNEL ENTRANCE

THE TREASURE CHAMBER

1

PLOTS AND PLANS

Joe's parents were arguing.

This was not unusual. Joe's father traveled on business for a large part of the year and Joe missed him terribly. But whenever he was home, his mom and dad would start arguments that sometimes lasted right up until the point when his dad left on business again.

Today's argument was about the surprise vacation his dad had arranged for the upcoming spring break. Joe sat at the kitchen table with his head down, pretending to do his homework, but he was listening carefully as his dad explained the plan.

"I've already told you, Penny," said his dad.

"It's a castle. A *real* castle. One of my clients bought it as an investment and he's partway through renovating it. He says we can use it over spring break, and he's given me the keys. It's got battlements and big fireplaces and even a moat." He moved closer to his wife and slipped an arm around her shoulder. "Come on, it'll just be the three of us. Imagine what a wonderful time we'll have."

Joe was already imagining what sort of fun

he could have in a castle. He pictured himself in a large banquet hall, throwing leftover bones to the dogs, or standing guard on the drawbridge with a sword in his hand. He wondered if the castle had suits of armor and swords and stuff like that. If it did, he was sure nobody would mind too much if he borrowed one for a bit of sword practice.

Unfortunately, Penelope Carter was not a castle sort of person. She did not much care for history, or places that were cold or damp, nor did she much enjoy spending time with "just the three of them." What Penelope Carter did like was sunshine and beaches and cocktails and glamorous people with impossibly deep suntans who wore designer clothes. She greeted her husband's plans with folded arms and a face like stone.

"Well, this is *typical* of you, Mike," she said. "You arrive home with some half-baked plan about going to a castle that you imagine we'll think is wonderful."

As it happened, Joe did think the plan sounded pretty wonderful but he knew that now was probably not the best time to say it.

"Did you stop to think about whether it was something *I* might want to do?" she asked. "Did you even bother to ask if *I* had anything planned for spring break?"

Mike Carter stared blankly at his wife. "Well, do you have anything planned for the break?"

"As a matter of fact, yes," said Penelope. "Maria Santorini called while you were away and invited us to spend the week on their yacht in the Mediterranean. Apparently, everyone who's anyone in fashion will be there. I accepted, of course."

Joe groaned inwardly at the thought of a week spent on a yacht with people he didn't know who talked about fashion the entire time.

His father wasn't quite ready to give up just yet. "But, Penny," he pleaded. "Couldn't we just—"

"No, we could not," said Penelope Carter firmly.

4

"You seem to forget that I had a career in fashion once, Mike. And if you think for one minute that I am going to miss the chance of catching up with my old friends to go and stay in a drafty old *castle*"—she spat out the word as though it tasted bad—"then you don't know me very well."

Mike Carter's shoulders drooped in defeat and Joe could see the castle vacation slipping away. He decided that now was the time to intervene. "But, Mom," he pleaded, "staying in a castle would be so cool. And it's totally educational. Besides, I really don't want to spend a week on a yacht."

"Well, that's very fortunate, Joseph," said his mother. "Because you are not invited."

Joe frowned. "What?"

"That's right, it's adults only, I'm afraid," said his mother. Joe's mouth dropped open. "Now don't pout, darling. You said yourself you wouldn't enjoy it for one minute. I called your grandmother and I've arranged for her to come and look after you for the week. She'll be here on

5

Saturday. I'm sure you'll both have a lovely time."

"But Mom—" began Joe.

Penelope Carter held up a solitary finger. "Sorry, but I'm not going to hear another word on the subject of castles. Your father and I are going to stay on a yacht, and you, Joe, are staying here with your grandmother and that's all there is to it. Now, if you'll excuse me, I'm going to pack."

Before either of them could say another word, Penelope swished out of the room, leaving Joe and his father to stare at each other helplessly.

"Sorry, Joe," said his dad. "I thought the castle would be a good idea."

"It *is* a good idea, Dad," said Joe. "Couldn't you persuade her to—"

"I don't think so," said his father. "Your mother intends to have her way on this one. I'd better go and help her pack."

After his dad left the room, Joe threw down his pen and let out a huge sigh. *A week at home with Nana*, he thought to himself. *Some spring*

break this is going to be. I bet nothing exciting
happens at all.

Joe spent the rest of the morning in his room,
sulking and imagining how thoroughly boring his
spring break was going to be with just him and
Nana. The house was filled with the sounds of
banging from the attic as his dad pulled down the
suitcases and there was a medium-sized argument
when his mom couldn't remember what she'd
done with her passport.

"Well, what do you expect, Mike," she shouted
as she went through the drawers in the study for
the third time. "It's been so long since I've been
anywhere, it's hardly surprising I can't find it."

Eventually, the packing was finished, the passport
was found, and the house became calm again. Joe's
dad appeared in his bedroom doorway, looking tired.
"We're just going to the store," he said. "Your mom
needs a few last-minute things for the vacation. We
shouldn't be more than an hour...or maybe two."

Soon after his parents had gone out, the phone in the hallway began to ring. And, as there was only one person who ever called them on the house phone, that meant Joe instantly knew who was calling.

He picked up the receiver. "Hello, Nana," he said.

"Joseph, is that you?" said a voice on the other end of the phone. "Can you hear me? It's Nana here. Speak up, boy!"

"Yes, I know it's you, Nana," said Joe. His grandmother was quite hard of hearing and her telephone voice always sounded like she was trying to communicate with someone at the bottom of a very deep well. He held the phone a little farther from his ear. "How are you?"

"Who am I? I've already told you who I am, you stupid boy. It's Nana," she snapped.

"Yes, Nana," said Joe, wishing he could start the conversation again. "I hear you're coming to look after me for the week."

"I'm supposed to be coming to look after you

for the week," said Nana. "But I completely forgot that I'd agreed to go to Littlehampton with Doris Flatley to visit her sister. I'll never hear the last of it if I don't go. Tell Penny that I can't come to you after all."

"Oh, I'm sorry to hear that," said Joe. He was genuinely sorry because he could imagine how badly his mother was going to take this news. "Mom and Dad are out shopping for some last-minute things," he said. "They're supposed to be flying to Italy tonight."

"Well, I can't help that," snapped Nana. "Besides, Littlehampton is a far nicer place than Italy. There's too many flies and they eat octopus, can you imagine that?"

Joe was confused. "They eat octopus in Littlehampton?"

"No, in Italy, you stupid boy," said his grandmother. "Tell Penny I'm very sorry but if I let Doris Flatley down she'll spread unpleasant gossip about me at the bridge club."

"Shall I get Mom to call you?"

"Certainly not," said Nana haughtily. "I'm going to bed early and I don't want to be disturbed. Now run along and don't forget to pass on my message. Goodbye."

The line had gone dead before Joe could answer. He replaced the receiver and rubbed his ear, which had become hot. Talking to Nana was like talking to an old lady version of his mother and just as tiring.

He really wasn't looking forward to passing on Nana's message. Either his mother would have to cancel her plans, or worse still, she might make him go with them. Either way, it was bound to make her furious and one way or another, she would find a way to blame it on him. If only he didn't have to tell them about Nana's phone call.

Then he paused. What if he didn't tell them? What if his parents just went to Italy and never got Nana's message? That wouldn't be so bad, would it?

An idea began to bloom in Joe's head and a slow smile crept across his face as he reached for his phone.

2

JOE'S NEWS

Charlie Wells looked in the fridge and sighed. One very squashy tomato, a dried-up block of cheese, and a pint of milk weren't going to go very far, she thought. She picked up the milk carton and sniffed, then recoiled quickly. She was still emptying the sour, clotted mess down the sink when her mother entered the kitchen.

"Charlie, darling, what *is* that awful smell?" Brenda Wells was a large woman who favored baggy harem pants, flouncy shirts, and open-toed sandals. She sat down at the kitchen table and closed her eyes while she rubbed her temples in small circles and made a faint humming sound.

"It's the fridge, Mom," said Charlie as she folded the empty milk carton and put it in the recycling. "We've got virtually no food in the house, and what we do have went bad last Christmas. I'll have to go to the store if we want any dinner tonight."

Brenda had stopped humming and was rummaging through a drawer crammed with screwdrivers, packs of playing cards, broken pencils, and old keys that no longer opened anything. "Ah, here we are," she said, pulling out a long packet of incense. "Lotus flower and jasmine—I knew I had some in here somewhere. This will drive away the smell." She lit an incense stick from the pilot light on the stove and began to waft thick curls of gray smoke around the room.

Charlie wrinkled her nose. She hated the smell of incense even more than the smell of sour milk. "That's it," she said. "I'm going to the store before we starve to death. What do you want to eat this weekend?"

Her mother stopped wafting the incense stick and sat down again. "Nothing for me, dear," she said. "You know I won't be here."

Charlie blinked. "What do you mean? Where will you be?"

Her mother flapped her hand impatiently. "I told you about it weeks ago, Charlie. I'm going on a yoga retreat with Miriam and the girls. I'll be there every day next week. I'm going to unblock my chakras and release my inner goddess."

Charlie frowned. "I have absolutely no idea what any of that means."

Brenda rolled her eyes. "It's part of my spiritual journey, darling," she said. "Don't look so worried, I'll be back in the evenings. I'll leave you some money for groceries and you've got my mobile number in case of emergencies. All you have to do is look after the house while I'm gone."

"Look after the house?" Charlie looked around at the peeling paint on the kitchen walls. "What do you think is going to happen to it? If anyone broke in here, they'd probably feel sorry for us and leave food."

Brenda rolled her eyes and stubbed out the incense stick in a saucer. "Please don't make one of your scenes, darling, I really have to be getting ready. Now, have you seen my prayer beads anywhere?"

After Brenda had wandered out of the kitchen, Charlie glanced over at her faithful dog, watching from his basket. "Well, Sherlock," she said. "I guess you and me are looking after ourselves over spring break. How do you feel about that?"

The little dog sat up, wagged his tail, and barked. Charlie grinned. "Yeah, it sounds like fun to me too," she said, reaching for her sneakers. "How about we stop off at the beach hut and see the others on the way back from the store? This could be the best break ever."

"So, how did you manage to do it?" Max placed a cup of hot chocolate on the table in front of Lucy, then sat down next to her on the cushions.

Lucy reached for the mug and gave an exasperated sigh. "Cross-country," she said. "Dad said it would be good to do some different types of training. He had me running up hills and across fields all last week. It was good fun, right up until the point where my foot went down a rabbit hole."

She stared glumly at her bandaged foot, resting on the cushions in front of her. "The doctor said it was just a bad sprain, but it will be at least six weeks before I can train properly again."

"Six weeks with your feet up," said Max. "It sounds great, Luce."

Lucy frowned. "It's not funny, Max," she said. "It's horrible for an athlete not to be able to train."

Max looked sheepish. "I'm sorry," he said. "I forget that not everyone hates physical exercise. Is there anything I can do to help?"

Lucy smiled. "Just keep me company for a bit

during spring break, otherwise I'm going to go stir-crazy."

"Sure thing," said Max, who liked nothing better than the prospect of staying indoors for a week. "Hey, perhaps I could teach you how to play *Warlocks and Dragons?*"

Lucy raised an eyebrow. "*Warlocks and Dragons?* I think I'd rather drink a mug of Joe's lumpy hot chocolate."

"Speaking of Joe, where is he?" asked Max. He checked the time on his phone and then looked out of the window and along the beach for any sign of Joe. "He said he'd meet us here in the beach hut twenty minutes ago."

It was a blowy day outside. The sea was gray and rough and only a few dog walkers had braved the windswept sands. Max was glad that the little beach hut had a heater and some comfortable seats to curl up on.

"What do you think this is about?" asked Lucy. "He sounded very excited in his message."

"You know Joe," said Max. "No doubt it will be something we could all end up in jail for."

Lucy smiled. Last Christmas, Joe had led them all on an adventure in a "borrowed" motorboat that had gotten them into trouble with the police. Although, she reminded herself, if he hadn't done it, they would never have caught the gang that was smuggling endangered animals.

"Here's Charlie and Sherlock," said Max. He stood back from the door as Charlie pushed her way in, carrying a plastic bag of groceries and closely followed by Sherlock. The little dog was delighted to see Max and Lucy, and leaped up onto the cushions to be petted.

Lucy winced. "Ow, Sherlock, be careful of my ankle," she said. But she laughed as he rolled

onto his back and allowed her to tickle his tummy.

"It's blowing like a hurricane out there," said Charlie. "Do we have any idea why Joe wanted to meet up? What's so important?"

"No idea," said Max, inspecting Charlie's shopping. "Do you have anything to eat in there? I'm starving."

"It's mostly dog food and fresh vegetables," said Charlie. "But there's some vegan chocolate. You could have some of that."

Max gave her a horrified look. "Vegan chocolate? That *can't* be good for you."

Charlie shook her head. "Real chocolate's not good for you, idiot," she said. "Here, try a bite, you might like it." She broke the bar and was handing it around when Joe arrived.

Joe looked like he had run all the way from his house. His face was bright pink, his hair was wild, and there was a huge grin plastered across his face. "Good," he said. "You're all here. I've got something really exciting to tell you."

"You're leaving town?" ventured Max.

Joe ignored him and pulled up a chair. "Not me—my parents are going away to spend a week on a yacht in Italy," he said. "They've just left for the airport."

"*That's* the really exciting news?" said Charlie. "Your parents are having a good time somewhere else?"

"No, of course not," said Joe. "The exciting news is that we all get to go and stay in the castle."

"I've seen your house, Joe," said Max. "It's big but I wouldn't call it a castle."

"No, no," said Joe, flapping his hands in frustration. "I mean a *real* castle. One with a moat and everything."

Lucy frowned. "Maybe you'd better start from the beginning."

So, he did. Joe told them about the castle that his dad's friend had let them borrow. He told them about the battlements and the fireplaces and the moat and how they would have the run of the place for the entire week. When he had finished, his eyes were shining and he looked even pinker in the face than before.

"Hold on a minute," said Lucy. "We can't just go and stay in a castle on our own. My parents would never allow it if there wasn't going to be an adult there."

"There will be," said Joe at once. "My nan said she'd be happy to come and look after us for the week. She's going to meet us there. It's all been arranged. Say you'll come, *please!*"

The others exchanged glances. They had past experience of Joe's grand plans and how they did not always work out as intended. But on the other hand, they had to admit that staying in a castle for a week did sound like the coolest thing ever.

"Well, me and Sherlock are in," said Charlie. "Mom's spending the week 'discovering her inner goddess,' so it's not like there's anyone to stop me."

Lucy was thoughtful. "Usually there's no way my dad would let me go away and interrupt my training," she said. "But I'm not going to be doing much of that for the next few weeks so I guess he might say yes."

"Great," said Joe. "Apparently there's a lake there, so you can tell your dad that you can go swimming." He turned to Max. "What about you, Max?"

Max pulled a face. "I don't know. Mom has a whole bunch of extra math lessons lined up for me over the break. I don't think she's going to let me go."

"How much math do you need to know, Max?" asked Joe. "I mean, I've never been able to remember what seven times eight is and it's not done me any harm."

"Perhaps," said Lucy, "it would help if you promised her that you'd do some work while you were away."

"Yes," said Joe. "And I could come and explain to her that my nan's going to be there."

Max blew out his cheeks. "I guess we can't lose

anything by giving it a try," he said. "But let me do the talking, Joe. After what happened at Christmas, my mom's convinced that you're a bank robber or something."

"Awesome," said Joe. "Then it's agreed. We're all going on our first vacation together. And we're going to have the best time."

"Not if Max keeps eating my vegan chocolate," said Charlie. She picked up the empty wrapper. "How did you manage to eat the whole bar?"

Max shrugged and wiped his mouth. "Actually, it's not that bad," he said. "I might consider becoming a vegan. Do they do vegan pork sausages?"

While Charlie went home to feed Sherlock, the others went to Lucy's house. As Lucy expected, her father was not enthusiastic about her doing anything to interfere with her training. "But, Dad," she pleaded as they sat in the front room, "it's not going to make any difference. I can barely walk at the moment."

Ken Yeung shook his head and sucked his teeth. "I don't know, Lucy," he said. "Training is about more than just being able to run. There's your diet to think of. You're bound to be eating junk food while you're away with your friends."

"My nan's a great cook," said Joe at once. "And Charlie's coming too. She has the healthiest diet of anyone I know. She's the only person I've met who eats vegetables with vegetables on the side."

In the end, it was Lucy's mother who intervened on her daughter's behalf. "Give the girl a break, Ken," she said to her husband as she handed around a plate of cookies. "Lucy's thirteen now and she deserves some time off with her friends after all the training you put her through. Joe's family are very nice people so I'm sure it will be all right. Then, when her ankle is better, she'll be ready to start training harder than ever. Won't you, Lucy?"

Lucy nodded eagerly and, after much deliberating about the dangers of "slacking off," her father agreed that she could go.

Max's mother, on the other hand, proved much more difficult to persuade. The three of them crowded in the doorway of her steamy kitchen to make their case as she chopped ingredients for a chicken stew.

"Absolutely no way!" she declared when Joe had explained about the castle. "Maximillian, if you think you are going to be running around in a castle with math grades as bad as yours, you've got another think coming." She hacked viciously at a bunch of spring onions as she spoke.

"Mom, my math grades aren't that bad," complained Max. "I got ninety-eight percent on that last paper."

"That's a whole two percent of improving you could be doing, Maximillian," she replied, shaking her kitchen knife in his direction, "instead of wasting the whole spring break."

"It wouldn't be wasted, Mrs. Green," chimed in Joe. "My dad said the castle was built in the eleventh century. The place is full of history.

It will be just like going on a school field trip, trust me."

"Trust you?" Joy Green's voice rose to a squeak and she glared at Joe. "And aren't you the boy who steals motorboats when no one is looking?"

Joe shrank back under Joy's fierce gaze. "I-I didn't exactly steal it..." he stammered. "I just kind of...borrowed it. Without permission," he added.

"Joe, just do me a favor and stop arguing on my behalf," hissed Max.

"We'll all be very responsible, Mrs. Green," said Lucy. "And Max could take some books with him and do some homework while he's there. I'll make sure he does it, if you like."

When Joy's eyes alighted on Lucy, her expression changed completely. "Lucy! Hello, my dear. I didn't see you standing there. Come in, come in. You two get out of the way and let her come through."

When she saw Lucy's bandaged ankle, Joy threw her hands up in horror. "Oh, good Lord, what have you done to yourself, child?"

"Don't worry, Mrs. Green, it's just a sprain. It'll be fine in a few weeks."

"Well, we must take care of you, child. Sit down, sit down." Joy made Lucy sit at the kitchen table while Max fetched another chair so she could rest her foot. Then she poured Lucy a large mug of tea and offered her a plate of cookies.

"So, how's your mother, dear?"

"She's very well, thank you, Mrs. Green," said Lucy, taking a cookie. She caught sight of Joe and Max looking on longingly and smiled.

"Tell your mother I'm going to bring some dresses into her shop for alteration. Such lovely silk things she has in there."

"She'll be very pleased to see you again."

Joy nodded happily and wiped her hands on a kitchen towel. She glanced at the two boys hovering in the doorway and looked thoughtful for a moment. "So, Lucy," she said, "if I let Max go on this trip, will you promise to make him do his math homework?"

"I promise, Mrs. Green," said Lucy solemnly. "I'll make him sit down and do it every day. I'll stand over him if necessary."

"Please, Mom," begged Max. "You're always saying I should get out more."

Joy looked at each of the children in turn and then threw up her hands in surrender. "Oh, all right," she said, exasperated. "But I'm counting on you, Lucy, to make sure he does his work. And Maximillian, you make sure you look after Lucy while she has a bad ankle."

But her words were lost in the delighted screams of the two boys as they jumped up and down in the hallway. Joy watched them for a moment and then let out a snort. "Heaven help me," she said. "I've become a soft parent."

3

THE NIGHT BEFORE

Charlie: Hllo—any1 thr?

Joe: Hi, Charlie

Charlie: Hw didit go?

Joe: Max and Lucy's folks both said yes

Charlie: rlly? thtS mazng—so wer all going? Fr real?

Joe: Looks like it. Excited?

Charlie: totlly

Lucy: Hi. I've just finished packing. Dad made me bring enough protein bars for a month.

Max: Great news, I love those things.

Lucy: You're only supposed to eat them if you're training.

Joe: Is everybody else packed yet?

Max: Mom made me bring every school book I own, plus she's cooked enough food for a small army.

Charlie: Ive gt sum spare clothes nd sum dog fd for S'lock

Max: Still using that old phone I see.

Charlie: Dnt nock it—it's a clssic

Lucy: What time is the train tomorrow, Joe?

Joe: 9:30—don't be late. It takes a couple of hours. We should be there by lunchtime.

Lucy: I'm so excited

Max: Me too.

Charlie: So is Srlock—he dsnt no whr we r gong but he knos smthng is up—hes ben lke a puppy all dy

Joe: I can't wait for us all to spend a week together without any grown-ups around.

Lucy: Apart from your nana, Joe

Joe: Yeah, that was what I meant. And we'll hardly notice Nana's there. It will be as good as being on our own.

Lucy: OK. I guess we'd better all get some sleep. Early start in the morning.

Charlie: Im going to bd nw—c u guys tmrw

Max: Yeah, me too. I need to summon my energy to lug all those books. Nite all.

Lucy: Nite everyone

Joe: See you tomorrow

Joe: You still there, Luce?

Lucy: What is it, Joe?

Joe: Do you think there will be any ghosts in this castle?

Lucy: Goodnight, Joe

Joe: Night

4

THE ROAD TO UFFORD

The following morning, just after nine, Lucy arrived at the station with her dad to find Joe, Max, and Max's dad already waiting for them on the platform. The two adults struck up a conversation about computers, a subject on which Max's dad was very knowledgeable, while the three children talked enthusiastically about the vacation.

"So where's your nan, Joe?" said Lucy, looking around.

"Oh," said Joe, startled. "Her house is nearer to the castle than ours. She's going straight there and she'll see us this evening." He looked at Max.

"Honestly, Max," he said. "I can't believe you're wearing a shirt and tie, *on vacation!*"

Max frowned and smoothed his tie down defensively. "It doesn't do any harm to be well presented," he said stiffly. "Something you could do well to learn, Joseph." As usual, Joe's clothes all bore designer labels, but they were rumpled and untidy and his shirt was hanging out of the back of his jeans.

Joe had brought a small bag for his clothes and an enormous cardboard box into which he appeared to have emptied the entire contents of his mother's fridge. His haul included pasta, bacon, eggs, bread, flour, milk, and a half-eaten bowl of trifle. "Well, we want to make sure we have plenty of supplies," he said when he saw Lucy staring at the box. "Castles always kept a lot of food in case they got besieged."

"And who do you think is going to besiege four kids and a dog?" asked Lucy, shaking her head.

Max had also brought plenty of food. As well

as his backpack, he had two large carrier bags filled with Tupperware containers, each one labeled with a day of the week. "After Mom agreed to let me go, she got worried that I wouldn't have enough to eat. She's cooked meals for every day that we're away."

"I'll help you out with that," said Lucy. "Your mom is the best cook in the world, or at least in Southwold." She looked up and down the platform. "Where's Charlie? That girl never turns up on time for anything. I hope she doesn't miss the train."

Charlie very nearly did miss the train. At half past nine, the engine swung into view around a bend in the tracks and slowed to a stop on the platform. The two adults helped the children onto their carriage, placing the food boxes in the luggage racks and settling them in a group of four seats around a table.

At the very last minute, just as the conductor was checking his watch, Charlie sprinted into view. She arrived at the carriage with seconds to spare, scooping up Sherlock and jumping onto the train moments before the whistle blew for departure. As the train began to shunt slowly out of the station, Lucy, Max, Joe, and Charlie gathered at the window to wave and shout their goodbyes.

"Goodbye!"

"See you in a week!"

"We'll send you a postcard."

"Bye!"

They waved madly to Lucy and Max's dads as the platform slid away then went to claim their seats at the window. They were on their way at last!

The train was largely empty, and they had a carriage almost to themselves. As soon as they were seated, Joe pulled out a thick stack of papers and spread them on the table. "This is the information my dad's friend sent him about the castle," he said. "It's called Ufford Castle, named after Baron Thomas Ufford, who built it in the eleventh century. That means it's"—he paused to count on his fingers—"a thousand years old."

The others pored over the badly photocopied pages. There were several smudgy pictures that showed a thick-walled tower built of gray stone. The walls were topped with broken battlements and there were narrow slit windows in the towers.

"Most of the old castle walls have fallen down now," said Joe. "But there's a big stone tower called 'the keep,' where the baron lived with his family. That's the part we're going to stay in."

"Well, I think it looks fabulous," said Lucy. "It looks just like a castle out of the history books." She ran her finger over the picture. "You could imagine knights in armor having jousting matches under these castle walls."

"It says here," said Charlie, "that the castle has its own grounds with a forest and a lake. It also says that there's lots of wildlife there." Her eyes gleamed. "It's a good thing I brought my binoculars with me."

"Do you think there might be some old weapons there that we could try out?" asked Joe. "I've always wanted to shoot a bow and arrow."

"Oh sure," said Max. "I can't see that ending badly at all." He checked his phone. "It says here that the train gets into Ufford Market station in about two hours. The castle is about eight miles from the station so I guess we'll need to get a bus or something."

"How about a swim in the lake as soon as we get there?" said Lucy. "I've been dying to get a bit of exercise since I hurt my ankle."

They all agreed this was an excellent idea and even Sherlock barked his approval, much to the annoyance of the other passengers. He had found a spot on the seat between Charlie and Lucy and was snuffling at the papers with interest. He had no idea where they were going but he was going with Charlie and her friends and that was really all that mattered to him. Wherever it was, Sherlock just hoped that they had seagulls there.

Joe put away the papers and stretched luxuriously in his seat. "This is going to be so cool," he said. "Just imagine, a whole week in a castle by ourselves, with no one to bother us."

The train drew into Ufford Market station just before lunchtime. It was a tiny station, with a white picket fence and flower boxes arranged along the platform. No one else got off the train and the driver had to wait for some time while Joe and Max struggled to unload their food supplies.

When the train had left, they dragged their luggage to the ticket office and piled it in a heap. "So, where do we get the bus?" asked Max as he collapsed, panting, onto the pile of bags.

"Did you say 'bus,' my dear?" asked a voice behind them. They turned around to see a red-faced woman emerging from the parcel office. She was carrying a large bag of animal feed and wore dungarees and heavy rubber boots. Her gray hair stood out around her head like wire. "You missed the bus not half an hour ago."

"Oh, no!" said Lucy. "When's the next one?"

"Not until tomorrow, I'm afraid," said the woman. Then she smiled. "Where is it you're going to?" They explained they were going to the castle and the woman nodded thoughtfully. "I reckon I could swing past the castle on my way to deliver this. If you don't mind riding in my old pickup truck, that is."

They assured her they didn't mind at all and followed her outside to where a battered red truck was parked haphazardly, half on the pavement. "Betty Grimes is the name," she said as she tossed the heavy feed bag into the back of the truck. "What are you all doing up at the castle, then? It looks like you've brought enough food for a month."

While Betty helped them with their luggage, they all talked at once, falling over each other to tell her about their vacation. She laughed and held open the passenger door. "Well, I reckon you'll find plenty to keep you in mischief up there," she said. "Just mind you watch out for old Black Shuck. They say he roams around those parts."

Lucy and Max climbed into the tiny back seats of the pickup while Charlie and Joe sat up front on the bench seat, with Betty. It was a tight squeeze and the truck smelled of horse manure, but they were all grateful for the lift. Sherlock sat on Charlie's lap with his paws on the dashboard while Betty steered the truck out of the station and through a pretty village of red-brick cottages with thatched roofs.

"Who's Black Shuck?" asked Max. "Does he have a house near the castle?"

Betty laughed heartily. "Dear me, no. Black Shuck ain't a person. He's a dog. At least he looks like a dog. Some folks say he's an evil spirit who takes the shape of a dog. Others say he's a hound from hell."

Joe swallowed. "A hound from hell?" he asked nervously.

"Either ways, you don't want to meet him on a dark night," said Betty.

"There's no such thing as hounds from hell," said Max. "That's just old superstition."

Betty nodded seriously. "Aye, there's plenty have thought the same thing. Right up until the moment when they felt Black Shuck's hot breath on their necks and saw his yellow eyes in the darkness."

Max looked unconvinced about the existence of Black Shuck but secretly all of them were feeling slightly chilled by Betty's story. They spent the remainder of the journey deep in thought as the countryside passed by. The sky was a clear china-blue and even though it was barely March, the sun was strong enough to make dappled patterns on the roadway through the new green leaves.

"Do you know if the castle has any dungeons?" asked Max. "All respectable castles should have a dungeon."

"Don't know about dungeons, young man," said Betty. "But there's a fair few old ruins around there for you to get your teeth into. There's even an old chapel on the grounds that's been there almost as long as the castle itself. I'd say you're going to have a high old time."

It seemed like the journey from the station went on forever, but at last, Betty's truck turned in to a long driveway, lined with trees. They followed the twisting lane for about a quarter of a mile and then suddenly, there in front of them, was Ufford Castle.

5

THE CASTLE

The castle stood in a field of long grass surrounded by mature forests of oak and beech. The crumbling exterior walls were made of gray stone, and in some places they were little more than rambling heaps of stonework, broken and flinty like old teeth.

At the top of the field, the old keep stood on a rise of ground. It was a thickly walled, octagonal tower with three smaller towers arranged around it. The tower was built from stone of two different colors and mossy plants grew between the gaps in the masonry. It immediately made Lucy think of the old tales she had read about knights and dragons and princesses.

Betty drove her truck up the narrow gravel drive and stopped at the base of the tower. There was no drawbridge but there was a small wooden footbridge across a wide moat that was partly filled with water. At the front of the tower was a set of stone steps with an iron handrail leading up to a heavy oak door.

They stumbled out of the truck, unable to take their eyes from the gray battlements looming above them. Two of the smaller towers appeared quite ruined, with broken archways and windows overgrown with ivy. But the main tower looked like it had been recently renovated with leaded glass panes in the windows and freshly repaired stonework.

"This place is awesome!" breathed Max.

"It's even better than in the pictures," said Lucy.

"And look!" said Charlie. "I can see a jackdaw's nest up there in one of the old towers."

Joe swelled with pride and puffed out his chest, as though the castle actually belonged to him. "Dad's friend has only renovated the one tower so far," he said. "But there's still plenty of room for all of us in there."

Betty helped them to heave their bags out of the truck and then dusted off her hands. "Well, have yourselves a grand time, m'dears," she said. "And remember what I said about watching out for old Black Shuck."

The children waved as she pulled down the drive and out of sight. When the noise of the truck's engine had faded, it felt suddenly quiet with only the wind in the trees and the sound of the jackdaws. "Well," said Joe. "Shall we go in?"

They picked up their luggage and walked the last few yards, crossing the bridge over the old moat. Lucy peered down at the green water where tiny silver fish caught the sunlight as they danced in and out of the weeds, and water boatmen skated across the surface.

"It's a shame it doesn't have a real drawbridge," said Joe, bouncing up and down on the boards. "We could pull it up and no one would be able to get to us."

"I think it's perfect just the way it is," said Lucy. She looked around. "Where's your nan, Joe? I can't see any sign of her."

"My nan?" said Joe. "Oh, her train doesn't come in until later. I'm sure she'll be here by this evening."

Lucy wondered how Joe's nan was going to get to the castle, given that there were no more buses but, before she could ask him, Joe had hurried across the bridge and was climbing the staircase to the big oak doorway. She frowned. Joe was behaving very oddly and past experience told her that usually meant he was up to something. But she quickly forgot her suspicions when she looked up at the walls of the old castle. The prospect of spending a whole week away with her friends was far too exciting to think of anything else. This was going to be the best spring break ever!

They followed Joe up the steps, Max carrying Lucy's bag so she could concentrate on getting up the stairs. Sherlock came last, his short legs only allowing him to take one step at a time. When they reached the top, Joe fumbled in his rucksack and pulled out an iron key, long as a ruler. It turned smoothly in the lock and the door swung open with a satisfying creak.

Inside, the air smelled cool and slightly damp as buildings made of old stone often do. They stepped into an enormous octagonal hall with a high ceiling supported by black timbers. The room was filled with an assortment of dark wooden furniture, squashy armchairs in faded red leather, a heavy dresser, and a grand piano covered with a red velvet cloth. The light came from four arched windows, swathed in heavy drapes. A faded Turkish carpet in reds and blues had been rolled out in front of a stone fireplace that was big enough to stand up in. In the center of the room, a monstrous brass chandelier hung on a long chain.

"This is the Great Hall," said Joe, consulting his papers. "It's where the lords and ladies would have spent most of their time."

"It's awesome," said Max. His voice was slightly echoey in the vastness of the hall. "Maybe we could light a fire while we're here?"

"We could roast a whole pig in that fireplace,"

said Joe eagerly. "Just like they did in medieval times."

"Ahem!" said Charlie. "Some of us are vegetarian, remember? But I suppose we could toast bread."

"Wow! Look at this," gasped Joe.

Hanging above the fireplace was a large shield painted with a black lion standing on its back legs and three red chevrons across the top. Behind the shield were two crossed swords, their handles wrapped in dark leather and their sharp edges gleaming in the half-light.

Joe's eyes had become as round as plates. "They're real swords," he gasped. "Just like knights in armor used to use. Here, help me get one down."

"Oh no you don't," said Lucy sternly. "Firstly, they don't belong to you and secondly, I can't think of a worse idea than letting you loose with a sword."

In another corner of the room, Max found a long bell rope that disappeared up into the ceiling. "What do you suppose this is for?" he asked.

Joe tore his gaze away from the swords and consulted his notes again. "It says here that they used to ring the bell to warn of the approach of an enemy," he said. "Apparently it still works."

Max grinned and grabbed the rope. "Shall I give it a pull?"

"Better not," said Charlie. "You might disturb the neighbors."

"Neighbors?" said Max. "I don't know if you noticed, but we're in a castle. It's not exactly semi-detached." But he let go of the rope anyway.

Downstairs they found a large, vaulted cellar that had been turned into a kitchen with a fridge, stove, and storage for their food supplies. There were tiny windows high up in the walls, which looked out at ground level outside, and a long kitchen table in front of another fireplace.

"Let's take a look at the bedrooms," said Joe. "I call the room at the top of the tower." He ran back up the winding staircase, followed by the others, all anxious to see where they would be sleeping.

On the first-floor corridor, four oak doors each led to a bedchamber with its own bathroom. In the first room they entered, they found a huge four-poster bed with thick velvet drapes that could be pulled around to conceal the person inside. There was another fireplace and arched windows that looked out across the forest.

"It's so beautiful!" Lucy looked around the room and hugged herself with delight. "Would anyone mind if I had this room? I've never slept in a four-poster before. I'd feel like a queen."

"I don't think Sherlock can make it up another flight of stairs," said Charlie. "Maybe we'll just take one of the rooms across the hall."

"That's okay," said Joe. "Me and Max will investigate the rooms upstairs. We might even be able to get out on the battlements from there."

Charlie took Sherlock to investigate the room across the hall while Lucy sat on the edge of her bed and tested it for softness. It was like sinking into a soft bale of cotton. She lay back on the soft quilt and smiled to herself, imagining a whole week without any training runs.

While the two boys crashed around upstairs, Charlie found her own room, which also had a four-poster bed with dark green drapes. While Sherlock snuffled in the corners, she put down her bag and looked around.

The bedroom was a million miles removed from her bedroom at home. It had bare stone walls and exposed beams and it looked just the way it might have a thousand years ago. She wondered how many people had slept in it before her and the thought made her shiver.

Her mother had once told her that really old buildings sometimes had something called an "aura." Charlie rarely paid any attention to the things her mom said and yet she couldn't shake off the strange feeling that this place gave her.

Just at that moment, Sherlock stopped scratching in the corner and began to growl suddenly. Charlie looked up and saw that he was facing the fireplace. His ears were back and his teeth bared as though he was growling at an intruder.

"What is it, boy?" she said, kneeling beside him. The hackles on Sherlock's neck were standing on end and his little body was shaking. He wouldn't take his eyes off the fireplace. "What have you heard in there?" she asked. "A mouse, maybe?"

She leaned in closer to the fireplace. At first, she could hear nothing at all, but then, very faintly, she thought she heard a distant clang of metal, drifting up through the fireplace. She leaned closer still and heard it again.

Charlie put her head almost completely inside the fireplace and there was no mistaking it now. She could hear the sound of steel on steel like a distant swordfight. At first she thought the boys had found some swords and were playing around with them. But the boys were upstairs and the sounds seemed to be coming from somewhere underneath the castle. It was as though an ancient battle was being fought right beneath her feet.

The noises stopped as suddenly as they had begun, and Charlie withdrew from the fireplace feeling cold all over. What she had heard was impossible, she told herself. They were the only people in the castle. And yet the sounds she had heard had been real, she was sure of that.

She hugged Sherlock closer, taking some comfort from his warmth. It couldn't be true, she thought. Surely the old castle wasn't haunted?

6

BLACK SHUCK

Lucy arrived downstairs with her swimming towel under her arm to find Max and Joe pretend-sword fighting around the kitchen table. "Shall we go and find the lake?" she asked. "Do you have your swimming things?"

"Already wearing them under my clothes," said Max with a smirk.

Lucy raised an eyebrow. "And you still put your shirt and tie back on?"

Charlie arrived in the kitchen with Sherlock. She looked pale and seemed distracted. Even Sherlock did not seem to be his usual bouncy self.

"Are you okay, Charlie?" asked Lucy. "You don't look well."

"What? Oh...yes, I'm fine thanks." Charlie forced a smile. "I guess it's just being in a strange place."

"You ready for a swim?" asked Joe. "Max is going in wearing his shirt and tie."

Charlie held up the small pair of binoculars that hung permanently around her neck. "I think I'll just do some wildlife spotting down by the lake, if you don't mind."

At the back of the kitchen, Max had discovered a shortcut to the gardens: a flight of stairs up to a small door that opened at ground-level outside. They gathered up their belongings and headed out in search of the lake.

The last of the afternoon sunshine was warm on their faces as they left the castle. They crossed the wooden bridge and headed down the hill toward the trees, walking slowly because of Lucy's ankle. Sherlock took off across the open grassland at top speed, changing direction frequently as though the field was filled with invisible rabbits that only he could see.

Lucy pointed to a grass-covered mound at the bottom of the field. "What's that?" she said. "It doesn't look natural."

The mound was about fifty yards long and its steep sides rose ten yards high so that it looked like a beached whale that had been covered with grass.

"I think I know what it is," said Joe excitedly. "It's called a barrow; it's where they used to bury the dead in ancient times. We learned about them in history."

"You mean there's bodies in there?" said Charlie, looking alarmed. "Bodies of people who died in the castle?"

"No," said Joe. "It's much older than that. That burial mound was probably here hundreds of years before the castle was built."

"Cool," said Max. "How about we go and investigate after our swim?"

They all agreed that the burial mound looked like an interesting place to explore, apart from Charlie, who remained very quiet. Joe pulled out his phone to take a picture of the mound and then frowned at the screen. "Hey, I have absolutely zero signal," he said.

Max pulled out his own phone. "Same here," he said, sounding dismayed. "There's no signal at all. How am I going to keep up with the latest *Warlocks and Dragons* news if I don't have the Internet?"

"I guess you'll just have to make do with living in a real castle," said Lucy. "Get over it, Max, it will do you good to live without your phone for a week."

Max shoved the phone back in his pocket and sulked as they tramped the rest of the way down the hill to the trees. The forest was dark and overgrown and the trees were alive with small birds making nests and furiously busy squirrels that Sherlock stared at longingly. Every few steps, Charlie would squeak with excitement and peer through her binoculars.

"Look over there..." she said in a stage whisper. "It's a hawfinch."

"You mean the brown thing?" said Max, squinting. "I thought it was a sparrow."

Charlie rolled her eyes. "Do you have any idea how rare they are?" she said. "Don't you care about wildlife at all?"

"All I care about right now is a dip in that lake," said Lucy. "Train journeys always make me feel sticky."

Joe led them through the last tangle of branches and they emerged at the edge of a wide lagoon. The pool was surrounded on all sides by large oak trees that cast a dappled light across the surface. The waters were clear, not green and slimy like the castle moat, and the air smelled moist and earthy.

Lucy clapped her hands with delight and sat down on a moss-covered rock to pull off her sneakers and socks. As soon as she stepped into the clear waters, she let out a sigh of pleasure.

"Oh, it's beautiful," she said. "I'm coming here every day to swim."

Joe and Max quickly peeled down to their swimming trunks and charged into the water, creating a huge wave that sloshed onto the opposite bank.

"Wait for me!" cried Lucy. She struggled out of her tracksuit and plunged in after the boys. The water was fresh and it made her gasp for breath, but she forced herself forward, breaking into a smooth crawl that cut through the water with barely a ripple. She smiled as she swam. For the first time in a week, the pain in her ankle was not bothering her.

Joe raced after her and, for a moment, the two swam side by side until Lucy increased her pace and left Joe behind. In the middle of the lake, she took a deep breath and dived down into the clear waters. The lake was deeper than it looked but Lucy was determined. She kept swimming down until her fingers made contact with the sandy bottom, then she turned and swam back up, breaking the surface only a few yards from Joe.

"It's like our own private pool," said Lucy. "Can you imagine if we lived here all the time?"

"I don't think I'd ever go anywhere else," said Joe. "Come on, Max, I could have swum all the way around the lake by now."

Max was doing a sedate breaststroke and carefully keeping his head above water. Lucy half expected him to still be wearing his tie. "There's nothing like a swim," he said, "for sharpening the appetite. Did anyone bring anything to eat? I'm starving."

Lucy laughed. "You'll have to wait until we get back."

"Time to get your hair wet!" yelled Joe. He made a huge splash that drenched Max, causing him to splutter and cough.

Max wiped his eyes and glared at Joe. "Right, you've asked for it."

Seconds later, the center of the lake erupted in a huge water fight, the three of them squealing as the water splashed over their heads. By the time they returned to the edge of the lake, they were glowing from the cold water and chattering excitedly.

They found Charlie sitting cross-legged on a rock with a big grin on her face. She had her binoculars in one hand and a small bird book in the other. "I've just seen a pair of lesser-spotted woodpeckers," she said excitedly. "And they were building a nest."

Sherlock had been amusing himself in the shallows, splashing up and down but not straying out of his depth, which was about four inches. When he saw the others returning, he splashed out of the water and greeted them by shaking doggy wetness all over them.

"Gah," said Max. "That's it. I've been dunked by Joe and now I smell like a wet dog. I'm going to get changed."

Max selected a thick bush and took his towel and clothes to get changed. The voices of the others faded quickly as he stepped into the undergrowth and he was suddenly struck by how dark it had become since the sun had lowered in the sky.

He glanced around and then started toweling

himself briskly, trying to get some warmth back into his muscles. He changed out of his swimsuit and pulled on a pair of dry shorts. Then he froze.

Something had moved in the bushes behind him. It was a soft movement of twigs and leaves, as though something was creeping through the forest and trying not to be heard. "Joe?" said Max as clearly as he could manage. "Joe, is that you?"

The sounds stopped. Max peered into the bushes but could see no more than a thick tangle of branches. Then he heard something else. The sound of breathing, hot and heavy, coming from the shadows behind him.

He spun around, holding up his towel defensively. "C-cut it out, Joe," he stammered. "I know it's you and I'm not frightened." Max swallowed and remembered the hair-raising tale that Betty Grimes had told them as they rode in her pickup truck.

This would not do, he told himself. Max prided himself on being a scientist. He believed in reason and logic. It was probably just some animal in the forest, a badger or a deer or something like that. He lowered his towel and leaned in closer to the bushes.

A pair of eyes appeared in the blackness, less than an arm's length from where he was standing. They were yellow and ringed with red fire, and the black pupils were focused intently on him.

Max forgot all about reason and logic. He turned and ran screaming from behind the bush, charging through leaves and branches like a blundering ox. His friends stared at him in surprise as he exploded from the bushes, panting and wild-eyed.

"Hey, nice shorts," said Joe, glancing down at Max's *Warlocks and Dragons* underwear. "What happened? Did you decide to go for a naked run in the forest?"

"B-B-B-Black S-Shuck," stammered Max.

Joe gave him a puzzled look. "What?"

"The d-demon-dog," gasped Max. "The one Betty told us about. I s-saw him. In the bushes." He turned and pointed, half expecting the demon-hound to burst out of the trees after him.

"Are you all right, Max?" asked Lucy. "You don't look too good."

"I'm telling you, I saw Black Shuck!" gasped Max.

"I thought you said there was no such thing as hounds from hell," said Joe, half laughing.

"That was before I saw a hound from hell," said Max. "His eyes were staring back at me from the bushes."

"It was probably just a deer," said Charlie. "I saw some tracks earlier. They come into the forest to look for acorns. I expect it was as scared as you were."

Max did not look convinced but he said nothing more. He shivered suddenly, realizing for the first time that it had turned quite cold.

"You should probably finish getting dressed," said Lucy. "And then we should go. It'll be dark before long."

"Can we still explore the barrow?" asked Joe. "There should be time."

Neither Max nor Charlie were very eager, but they didn't argue.

Max had got over his fright and was beginning to feel foolish. But as soon as they left the forest, he started to feel better. The sun was setting and the whole field was filled with red and gold light. It took them a while to reach the barrow, which was farther away than it had first appeared. Joe immediately ran up the side to the top of the grassy slope, closely followed by Sherlock.

"Come on, you varlets!" he cried to the others. "Come and challenge me for the castle if you dare."

"Show a bit of respect, Joe," said Lucy. "There's someone buried in there."

"I don't think so," said Max. He was standing at the end of the mound and looking through a low stone archway that led to the dark interior. "It looks to me like it's empty."

Joe got down off the mound and crouched to peer inside. "Shall we go in?"

"No!" said Max and Charlie simultaneously.

They glanced at each other, then looked away, embarrassed.

"And who are *you*, exactly?" asked a loud voice from behind them. They all turned to see a tall woman striding up the path toward them. She had iron-gray hair and Joe guessed she was about the same age as his nan. She wore a waterproof jacket with leather riding boots and carried a stout stick.

Sherlock decided the woman had come close enough. He placed himself between the children and the woman and began to bark, loudly and continuously. The woman did not flinch. She looked down at the little dog and held up one finger.

"Sit!" she said firmly.

Sherlock stopped barking immediately. For a moment he seemed confused; he looked around at Charlie, then at the woman, and then sat down obediently.

"How did you do that?" asked Charlie in astonishment. "He doesn't do that for anyone but me. He doesn't even do it for me most of the time."

"All dogs are pack animals," said the woman. "You just need to show them who's in charge of the pack." She bent down to pat Sherlock and he licked her hand as though he had known her all his life. "Now then," she said as she straightened up. "What are you all doing here? You do know this is private property?"

"We're staying at the castle," said Lucy.

"We're on vacation," added Joe.

"Ah, yes," said the woman, leaning on her stick. "You must be the children Betty told me about when she dropped off my animal feed." She looked around. "Surely you're not here by yourselves?"

"My nan's coming to look after us," said Joe quickly. "She'll be here later."

"I see." The woman looked them up and down. She had an intense gaze and a strong face and looked like she took no nonsense from anyone. "Well," she said eventually. "It seems that we're going to be neighbors, for the next week at least. My name is Mary Pollock," she said. "I live on the other side of the forest, in one of the estate cottages."

"It's nice to meet you, Mrs. Pollock," said Lucy.

"*Miss* Pollock," said the woman sharply. "Never married. Don't care to."

"Have you lived here long, Miss Pollock?" asked Lucy.

"All my life," she replied.

"Then you must know a lot about the castle," said Max.

Miss Pollock gave a curt nod. "I pride myself on being something of a local historian. I'm writing a book about Sir Thomas Ufford, who built the castle in the eleventh century. What do you want to know?"

"Is there anyone buried in here?" asked Joe, pointing to the burial mound.

Miss Pollock glanced at the barrow. "Once upon a time, maybe," she said. "This is a Saxon burial mound, otherwise known as a barrow. There are dozens of them around here but a barrow of this size would have been made for someone of great importance. A local baron perhaps, or maybe even a king."

"A king?" breathed Joe, hanging on Miss Pollock's words.

Miss Pollock bent down to look through the stone archway. "Unfortunately, as you can see, this tomb was long ago emptied by grave robbers. Whoever was put in here would probably have been buried with their armor, their swords, and whatever wealth they possessed." She tapped on the stones with her stick. "But it's quite empty now. You can go inside and have a look if you like."

"Er, perhaps when there's a bit more light," said Max quickly.

Charlie spoke up. "What I'd like to know," she said, "is whether there are any ghosts in the castle." The others turned to look at her curiously. It was not a question that any of them had expected Charlie to ask.

"Ghosts?" said Miss Pollock. "Oh, there's plenty of ghosts, alright. The castle is nearly a thousand years old and there's more than a few lords and ladies that have met their ends there. But there were ghosts and legends about this part of the country even before the castle was built."

"You mean like the legend of Black Shuck?" said Max.

"Yes, I've heard that one," she said. "But there are others too." She paused and looked around for somewhere to sit, finally selecting a low rock near the entrance to the tomb. "For instance," she said when she was settled, "did any of you ever hear about the legend of Ragnar's Gold?"

7

RAGNAR'S GOLD

Joe's eyes grew round. "Who was Ragnar?" he said.

"And more importantly, where's his gold?" asked Max eagerly.

Picking up on the general excitement, Sherlock stood up and began to bark, but when Miss Pollock raised her finger for silence he quickly sat down again and was quiet. "Patience, patience," said Miss Pollock. She checked her watch. "I suppose I have a little time to tell the story," she said. "But you must promise to sit down and be still. And above all, absolutely no interrupting."

They promised they would do as she asked

and sat down on the grass around Miss Pollock's feet. The sun was just setting, bathing everything in a deep red glow and Miss Pollock's eyes gleamed as she settled back on the stone and began the story.

"A long time ago," she began, "long before the castle was here, long before England was even one country, the countryside around these parts was prey to invaders from a land across the sea. A place they called Scandinavia."

"Vikings!" interrupted Joe, forgetting his promise. "They came from Scandinavia."

Miss Pollock silenced Joe with a frown. "It was indeed the Vikings," she said. "They came across the sea in longships. Fierce warriors with red hair and battle axes, they found a land that was ripe for the taking. There were wealthy monasteries along the coast, filled with precious artifacts and farms with stores that overflowed with food. The people who lived here were peaceful and had no experience of war.

"The raids became steadily more daring and more bloodthirsty under the leadership of a Viking king named Ragnar Lothbrok. Ragnar made many successful raids along this part of the coast and he and his clan became very wealthy. But it wasn't enough. Ragnar hatched a bold plan to invade England and take it for his own. He assembled a huge army and landed his boats on the coast not far from here. They worked their way inland, stealing and killing as they went, and it seemed as though no one could stop him."

The children were absolutely quiet as Miss Pollock was speaking and even Sherlock seemed to be lapping up her words. "But there was one person who tried," she continued. "A young boy king named Edmund who came to the throne when he was just fourteen years old. Edmund was determined to defend his country against the invaders. He assembled his army and pushed the Vikings back in a series of daring and bloody battles.

"Finally, Ragnar and his armies retreated all the way back to the coast. Edmund knew that all it would take was one last effort to drive the enemy out of England. And so, on a spring day nearly thirteen hundred years ago, the two armies prepared to meet in battle right on this very spot."

Joe's eyes had grown so wide that they looked like they might fall out of his head. "A real battle? Right here?" he said. "What happened? Did the boy king win? Did the Vikings get away? What happened to all the gold they took?"

Miss Pollock frowned. "I'm getting to that part," she said sharply. She settled back on her stone. "Things had not been going well for Ragnar. He knew that if he was defeated then all of the gold he had stolen would be lost. On the night before the battle, he buried his treasure in a secret place. He thought that if they lost the battle and were forced out of the kingdom, they would be able to come back for it at another time."

Miss Pollock became very serious. "The next

day the battle was long and bloody, and things went badly for both sides. Ragnar Lothbrok was killed in the fighting and the boy king was mortally wounded with an arrow. But eventually the Vikings were driven into the sea and a long period of peace reigned over the land."

"What happened to the treasure, Miss Pollock?" asked Lucy. "Was it ever found?"

Miss Pollock shrugged. "No one is sure," she said. "There are no records of where Ragnar buried his treasure nor are there any accounts of the treasure ever having been found. Some people say that Edmund and Ragnar are still fighting over the gold from beyond the grave and that on a quiet night you can hear the sounds of battle from under the ground."

"How amazing would it be if we could find some buried treasure while we were here?" said Joe.

"That may not be such a good idea," said Mary Pollock. "According to local legend, before he died, Ragnar prayed to the gods to protect his treasure.

His prayer was heard by Odin, the king of all the gods, who set his own dog to guard over the gold, a black demon-hound that roamed the land and would kill anyone who tried to steal it."

Max gasped. "You're talking about Black Shuck!" he cried. "A black dog with red and yellow eyes." He shivered as he thought of the apparition he had seen in the forest.

Miss Pollock nodded. "There are people around here that believe they've seen Black Shuck." She snorted. "Of course, it's all nonsense, if you ask me."

Joe's eyes were shining. All through Miss Pollock's tale he had sat, open-mouthed, hanging on every word. "That's a fantastic story," he said. "Can you tell us another one?"

"Heavens, no," said Miss Pollock. She stood up abruptly and checked her watch. "I need to get back and feed my horse, and you need to run along. No doubt your grandmother will be looking for you very soon."

The children realized it had become quite dark while they had been listening to Miss Pollock's story. They stood up stiffly and stretched their limbs as Sherlock uncurled himself and wagged his tail, glad that they were on the move.

"Thank you for the story, Miss Pollock," said Lucy. "I expect we'll see you at some point over the next week."

"I expect so," said Miss Pollock. "Well, enjoy yourselves and don't worry too much about Black Shuck. I've lived here for sixty years and I've never seen him. Good night!"

They waved goodbye to Miss Pollock and watched her stride away down the hill before beginning the long plod back to the castle. "She's a strange lady," said Joe as they walked. "But that was a great story."

"Well, I thought she was nice," said Lucy. "And she certainly knew a lot about local history."

"Sherlock liked her," said Charlie. "And he's always a very good judge of character."

"You don't think it was true what she said about Black Shuck, do you?" asked Max, looking back over his shoulder.

"Are you still going on about that?" Joe laughed. "I thought you didn't believe in that sort of thing. Personally, I'd love to see a demon-hound or hear Ragnar and Edmund doing battle."

"Are you all right, Charlie?" asked Lucy. "You look really pale."

"What? Oh, yeah, I'm fine. Just a little cold that's all," Charlie said. She dug her hands into her sweatshirt pockets and stomped ahead so that Lucy couldn't ask her any more questions.

Charlie had been very quiet all through Miss Pollock's story and she could not stop thinking about the strange noises she had heard in her room. She knew there was no such thing as ghosts really, but the sounds of crashing steel from the chimney had sounded very much like the sounds of battle that Miss Pollock described. Now, as they drew closer to the castle, the prospect of spending the night in that old room began to fill her with dread. She wondered how she could make an excuse to sleep somewhere else without being ridiculed by Joe.

By the time they all arrived back at the castle it was completely dark and they were ravenous. They headed straight for the kitchen and Joe looked inside the fridge thoughtfully. "I brought some burgers," he said. "And there's veggie burgers for Charlie. Why don't you guys go and finish unpacking while I start cooking?"

"Sounds good," said Charlie. "But I think I'm going to go outside with Sherlock first. I heard an owl earlier and I thought I'd see if I could find it."

As Charlie went up the stairs to the back door, Joe examined the rest of their food supplies. "I could make some fries and baked beans too and we could eat the remains of the trifle afterward," he said. "How does that sound?"

Max groaned and clutched his stomach. "It sounds like it might take forever," he complained.

"If I don't eat now, I think I might faint." He tugged on his waistband. "Look, my pants are getting looser already!"

Joe laughed. "I'll have it ready in less than an hour," he said. "Even you can wait that long. Here, have one of these to keep you going." He reached into the fridge and tossed Max an apple.

"Food in an hour would be perfect," said Lucy. "That gives Max plenty of time to get some math homework done."

Max's jaw dropped open. "What? You can't be serious, Luce? Not tonight."

"I promised your mom," said Lucy. "And I mean to keep my word, or she'll never trust me again."

Max protested but Lucy would have none of it. Ignoring his pleas, she forced him upstairs to the Great Hall and installed him at an old wooden writing desk. "I'll let you off with just one hour tonight," she said, "then you can come downstairs and have something to eat with a clear conscience."

"My conscience is fine, Luce," he said. "Believe

me, I feel no guilt whatsoever about skipping math for one night."

Lucy waited until she had seen him open his books and start some of his math exercises. Then she returned to the kitchen wearing a determined expression. There was one other person she had to tackle now.

She found Joe frying burgers in the kitchen. "So, where is she, Joe?"

Joe looked up and blinked at Lucy. 'Where's who?'

Lucy crossed her arms and frowned. "Don't play innocent with me," she said. "I'm talking about your nan. She's still not here."

Joe shifted uncomfortably and turned his attention back to the burgers. "Oh, that," he said. "She probably just got delayed. I'm sure she'll be here later, or maybe even tomorrow."

"There are no more trains tonight," said Lucy. "And there aren't any taxis from the station either. And you keep forgetting that she's supposed to be here." She stood right beside him so that he couldn't ignore her. "Be honest, Joe. She's not coming, is she? She was never coming."

Joe looked at Lucy and his bravado crumbled. He made a pained face and shrugged. "I *wanted* her to come with us," he said. "But she was going to Littlehampton and it seemed like such a waste to let this place go empty for a week. I didn't think anyone would mind us staying here by ourselves. What harm could it do?"

"What harm could it do?" exploded Lucy. "If you didn't think anyone would mind, why didn't you tell your parents what you were planning? More importantly, why didn't you tell *us*?"

Joe was looking decidedly sheepish now. "It's not so bad here, is it?" he asked weakly.

"It's wonderful here!" said Lucy, exasperated. "But we really can't stay in someone else's house without their permission. And I'm really angry that you made me lie to my parents. I'm sorry, Joe, but we have to leave."

Joe looked aghast. "Leave? But we only just got here."

Lucy was adamant. "It's not right, Joe," she said. "I can't believe you lied to us again, after everything that happened at Christmas. First thing in the morning we should get the train back to Southwold."

Now Joe was beginning to look panicked. "Look, Luce," he said. "It's not as bad as all that. Why don't we all have something to eat and then sleep on it?

I'm sure in the morning you'll feel differently."

"No, I won't," insisted Lucy. "It's wrong for us to stay here when we don't have permission. Tomorrow we'll—"

Lucy stopped mid-sentence and frowned. From somewhere outside the castle walls came the most blood-curdling scream. A moment later there was a clatter of feet on the staircase and Max appeared in the kitchen, looking terrified.

"Did you hear that?" he said. "That screaming came from outside. I think it's Charlie!"

8

THE FIRST CLUE

The three friends raced up the stairs to the back door. Joe paused long enough to retrieve a flashlight hanging from a nail before they ran outside. He shone the flashlight around, illuminating broken stone walls, bushes, and tufts of grass. But there was no sign of Charlie.

"She must be here somewhere," said Max. "I'm sure that was her screaming."

A second scream rang out, echoing off the castle walls. "I'm over here, somebody help me!"

"It *is* Charlie," said Lucy.

"It came from that direction," said Max. "Behind the ruined tower."

They followed the light of Joe's flashlight around the walls of the Great Keep, until they reached the ruined tower they had seen from the driveway. It was much more derelict than the one they were staying in. The roof was gone and the walls had partly collapsed. Ivy twisted through broken arches and the ruined stone steps led to nowhere.

"Charlie!" shouted Joe. "Where are you?"

"Over here," came back Charlie's voice. "Please hurry! It's Sherlock."

On the far side of the tower, they found Charlie on her hands and knees scratching at the dirt beneath a thick bush. "What's happened?" asked Lucy. "Where's Sherlock?"

"He's under there," sobbed Charlie. "We were looking for the owl but Sherlock startled a rabbit and he chased it under this bush. He began digging, but then he just disappeared. Please help me, I can hear him whining somewhere. I think he might be hurt."

Charlie was in floods of tears and her bare

hands were dirty and scratched where she had been trying to dig with them.

"Here," said Joe. "Let me have a look with the flashlight."

While Lucy gently moved Charlie aside, Joe kneeled down to take a look under the bush. Among a tangle of branches and old roots he could make out some rough wooden boards, partially hidden by dirt. There was a hole at the edge of the boards, just large enough for a small dog to have slipped through.

"Help me clear some of these branches," he said. "I think Sherlock's fallen down that hole."

They used their feet to trample some of the thicker branches, then Charlie wrapped her jacket around her hands and pulled away as many of the smaller branches as she could manage. When they had finished, their hands and arms were covered in scratches and Joe had a graze across one cheek.

Their efforts had revealed a round wooden cover.

The wood looked ancient and rotten and when
Joe pulled at it, the boards broke easily in his
fingers, uncovering a deep shaft, two yards across
and lined with bricks.

"It looks like a well," said Max. "It must be where the people in the castle got their water."

"Oh, no!" cried Charlie. She looked truly panicked now. "Please say Sherlock hasn't fallen all the way in?"

Joe pulled away the last of the boards and they crowded around as he shone his flashlight down the hole. The first thing they saw was a pair of bright eyes looking back at them from the darkness.

"Sherlock!" cried Charlie. The little dog was stuck about three yards down the hole. He was standing on a tangle of branches and broken wood that partially blocked the shaft and which looked like it might give way at any moment. He was frightened and shaken but yelped with delight when he saw them.

Down one side of the hole, thick iron staples had been driven into the brickwork that were clearly meant to act as a ladder. "I have to get down there," said Charlie desperately. She swung her legs over the side of the hole and it was all the others could do to hold her back.

"Wait, Charlie," said Lucy. "Even if you reach Sherlock, you won't be able to carry him back up that ladder. We'll need a rope to pull him out."

"I saw a rope earlier," said Max, "in the kitchen cupboard where the tools and cans of paint are. I'll go and get it." Using his phone as a flashlight, Max hurried back the way they had come, then returned a few minutes later with a thick coil of hairy rope slung over his shoulder. "I think this is long enough to pull Sherlock up if someone ties one end around him," he explained. "So, who's going down?"

"Me," said Charlie at once. "I'm the smallest and I'll fit down the hole the easiest. Plus, he's my dog." She glared at each of them in turn and no one dared to argue. Then she took a deep breath, wiped her hands on her sweatshirt, and swung her legs over the side. They watched her climb carefully down the well, using the iron staples as rungs. As soon as Sherlock realized that it was his beloved Charlie who was coming to fetch him, he began to bark excitedly.

"Calm down, and keep still, you stupid dog," she said. "Or you'll end up going all the way to the bottom."

She drew level with the narrow ledge where Sherlock was standing. Holding the ladder with one hand, she did her best to keep Sherlock calm, afraid that his rickety platform could give way at any second.

"All right," she called out. "Send the rope down."

Max and Joe unraveled the long rope and lowered it into the hole. Charlie reached the rope beneath Sherlock's front legs, then his back legs, hooking her arm through the iron rungs so that she could use both hands to tie the knot. She pulled it tightly so that Sherlock let out a little whimper. "It's for your own good, you silly dog," she said. "I don't want to lose you now. Okay," she called to Max when she was ready. "Pull him up."

Max and Joe heaved on the rope and immediately Sherlock was hauled up the side of the well, his four paws hanging comically beneath him as he looked around with a puzzled expression. The boys kept hauling, hand over hand, until Sherlock's back and shoulders appeared at the top of the well. While Max held the rope, Joe quickly reached in and pulled the little dog to safety.

Sherlock shook himself vigorously as Joe removed the rope.

"Do you have him?" called Charlie. "Is he all right?"

"He's fine," yelled back Joe. "You can come up now."

But as Charlie started back up the ladder, her foot slipped on the wet metal rung. For a moment she dangled in the air, just holding on with her hands. Her feet struggled to find a grip and she kicked against the rough platform of branches. There was a loud crash and a rumble from inside the well.

"Charlie!" called out Max. "Are you all right?" He shone the flashlight down the well and for

a moment he could see nothing but dust. Then he saw Charlie holding on to the ladder just below him.

"I'm fine," she said. "It was just the old branches that Sherlock was standing on. They've fallen all the way to the bottom."

"You nearly gave me a heart attack," said Joe. "Get out of there quickly, before anything else happens."

"Wait a minute," said Charlie. "There's something here." Charlie was peering intently at a section of the brickwork. "There's a hole in the wall," she said. "I couldn't see it before because the sticks were in the way. It looks like there's something inside." Gripping the ladder with one hand, Charlie reached into a hole in the shaft wall. The hole seemed quite deep and Charlie's arm disappeared up to the elbow. Max heard the scraping of metal on stone.

"I've got it!" she cried. "I'm coming up."

They watched Charlie climb awkwardly with

the heavy bundle in her hand. When she got to the top of the well, she handed it up to Max. "Here, take this."

Charlie clambered out of the well and Sherlock fell on her, yelping and whining and covering her with wet licks. She held him at arm's length to check him for any injuries and then hugged him tightly. "Oh, Sherlock," she cried, "don't ever do that to me again. I thought I'd lost you for good that time."

The others made a fuss of Sherlock as he licked each of their faces in turn. "He doesn't seem to be too worried," said Joe. "Do you think dogs forget about things right after they've happened? Like goldfish."

Charlie gave him an incredulous look. "Goldfish? Dogs are nothing like goldfish, Joe!" Then she gave him a half smile. "But thank you for helping me to rescue Sherlock."

"Well, we couldn't exactly leave him, could we?" said Lucy. "It would have been as bad as leaving one of us down there." She tickled Sherlock affectionately under his chin.

"Hey, what is that thing?" asked Max. He had turned his attention to the loose bundle of rags that Charlie had brought up. The bundle was about the size of a shoebox and surprisingly heavy.

"I'm not sure," said Charlie. "It was pushed well back, as though someone wanted to keep it hidden."

"It's too dark to look at it properly out here," said Max. "Let's take it inside. Besides, I'm half starved. How long until dinner's ready, Joe?"

Joe slapped a palm to his forehead. "Oh, no!" he gasped. "My burgers!"

By the time they returned to the kitchen, the smoke alarm was beeping frantically and the air was full of black smoke. Joe's burgers looked like four black hockey pucks in the bottom of the frying pan. "I guess dinner might be a little later than I'd planned," he sighed. He dumped the burgers into the trash can and retrieved four fresh ones from the fridge.

While Joe started cooking again, Charlie fetched a can of dog food and emptied it into a dish for Sherlock. She stood over him anxiously while he buried his nose and wolfed the food down hungrily.

"Well, his ordeal doesn't seem to have affected his appetite," said Lucy. "I think he's going to be okay, Charlie."

Max placed the heavy bundle on the kitchen table and pulled at the cloth wrappings, which broke apart easily in his fingers. "Whatever this is, I'm guessing it's been down there for a very long time."

Eventually he uncovered a small black box made of painted metal with a tight-fitting lid. "You don't suppose Ragnar's Gold is in there, do you?" asked Joe breathlessly.

"I don't think so," said Max. "Look." Painted on the top of the box in faded gold letters was one word, *Ufford*, followed by the date, *1758*.

"Thomas Ufford is the name of the man who

built the castle," said Lucy. "Maybe this box belonged to one of his descendants?"

"Maybe they put the treasure in here," said Joe, who was not quite ready to abandon the idea that the box might be full of gold. "Open it, Max."

"We should probably wait," said Lucy. "By rights the box belongs to the person that owns the castle, not us."

"Well, we're not going to steal it," said Max. "And I'm sure they wouldn't mind if we just had a peek." Joe and Charlie nodded in agreement and Lucy had to admit that she couldn't bear the thought of leaving it unopened either.

Very carefully, Max tried to lift the lid of the box. It was stiff and well-sealed with rust. After a few tries he pulled a multi-tool device from his pocket and selected a short penknife blade.

Joe marveled at the gadget in Max's hand. "Do you carry that thing everywhere with you?" he asked.

"Of course," said Max, inserting the blade under the edge of the lid. "Doesn't everyone have one of these?"

"That boy is such a geek," said Lucy, shaking her head.

The lid of the box sprang free with a scraping, metallic noise and the four friends crowded around it. "Please say it's full of gold," said Joe. "Or even just half-full would be okay."

A musty smell rose from the box as Max lifted the lid. Inside he found a small leather-bound notebook, pulpy from the damp, which he set on one side. The bottom of the box was lined with a thin sheet of reddish-brown metal. There was nothing else.

"Is that it? I was hoping for a few rubies at the very least," said Joe. "I'm going to finish making dinner." He stomped off to tend to his burgers.

Lucy picked up the notebook and prised the pages apart carefully. She knew that very old books sometimes crumbled away when they were opened, but it seemed well preserved, despite its age.

Inside, the pages were covered with spidery brown handwriting, filling every available space. Lucy squinted hard at the writing, but it made no sense to her. "I can't understand a word of this," she said. "It looks like it's written in code."

"It's written in Latin," said Max, looking over her shoulder.

"How do you know that?" asked Lucy.

"My mom thought it would be a good idea for me to learn Latin at one point," said Max. "She said all the best-educated people know Latin."

"So, you can actually read this?" said Charlie.

"Nah, not a word," said Max. "I just used to sit at the back of the class playing on my phone. After all, who needs to speak to a dead Roman? But I think I've still got a Latin dictionary on my phone somewhere. I might be able to translate a few words."

"That won't do us much good," said Lucy,

turning the pages of the notebook. "There's loads of this stuff; it would take forever. Look, there's drawings in here as well."

She paused at a scratchy ink sketch showing an outdoor scene with a low grassy mound in the foreground. "I recognize that," said Charlie. "It's the burial mound."

"There's more here," said Lucy, turning another page. "Look, that's a drawing of the castle and here's a picture of an old church. Someone was making a lot of detailed notes about something. If only we could read what it says."

The last two pages of the notebook were blank apart from a small inscription. Max squinted at the letters and read them out in a clumsy accent.

"*Hic est dimidia pars historiae Vicingorum auri. Sed si moriturus, secretum mecum, ad sepulchrum ibit*," he read. "And there's a name too, Cecilia Ufford—1761." His jaw dropped open and he looked up at his friends. "Guys, I think this might be important."

"For all you know it could be a three-hundred-year-old recipe for cupcakes," said Charlie.

"No," said Max. "Look at this word, *Vicingorum*. That can only mean 'Viking.' And here, where it says *auri*, I'm pretty sure that means gold!"

The friends fell silent as the enormity of what Max had said began to sink in.

Joe returned from the stove, wiping his hands on a tea towel. "Whoa, hold on a moment," he said. "Viking gold? Are you saying this message could tell us how to find Ragnar's Gold?"

"We don't know that," said Lucy. "We have no idea what it says. It could be something completely unimportant."

"If it's so unimportant then why go to so much trouble to hide it?" asked Max.

"There's something else in here," said Charlie. She reached into the box and took out the thin sheet of brown metal lining the bottom. "It looks like a sheet of copper."

When Charlie placed the metal sheet on the

table, they could see a pattern of engraved lines on its surface. The lines were scratchy and seemed to make little sense; they looked like the random doodles of a five-year-old.

"That's no help either," said Charlie. "Is it meant to be a map?"

"It doesn't look like a map," said Max. "And it's not writing either." He took a picture of the metal sheet with his phone and magnified it to examine it more closely.

After a few minutes he put down his phone and rubbed his eyes. "I'm getting too tired to think about any of this," he said. "It's probably just some sort of ancient joke and we've all fallen for it."

"Let's have some food before we do any more thinking," said Joe. He placed a large plate of buttered bread on the table and then began to ferry plates from the stove, loaded with burgers, fries, and beans.

There were groans of delight from around the table and for a moment, the mystery of the strange box was forgotten. "Oh, wow!" said Max, talking through a mouthful of burger. "If I was any more hungry, I think I might have eaten Sherlock. Just kidding," he added, when he caught the look on Charlie's face.

"Perhaps we should try to find out something about Cecilia Ufford," said Joe, slapping the ketchup bottle over his chips. "If we knew who she was then we might have a better idea of what she was looking for."

"Miss Pollock might know something about her," said Max. "First thing tomorrow we should go and ask her."

Lucy pushed her plate aside and wiped her mouth. Her face was serious. "We aren't going to talk to Miss Pollock or anyone else tomorrow," she said. "Tomorrow morning, we need to pack our bags and go home."

Charlie and Max looked at her incredulously. "What are you talking about?" said Max. "We only just got here."

"Joe knows why we can't stay," she said.

Joe stared down at his plate.

"It turns out we don't have permission to be here. Joe lied about it, just like he lied about his nan coming to look after us."

Charlie and Max looked stunned. "Are you serious?" said Charlie. "You mean Joe told us another one of his fibs? And we believed him?"

Poor Joe looked thoroughly miserable. "I'm sorry," he said. "I thought it would be fun if we all came to stay in a castle. I didn't think you'd mind once you saw how cool it was."

Max rolled his eyes. "Oh, that's just great," he said. "After all the persuading I had to do with my mom. She's never going to trust anything I say after this."

They lapsed into an unhappy silence as the prospect of an exciting week slowly evaporated. For the sake of having something to do, Joe began to clear away the dirty plates. Then he glanced down at the box and paused. Putting down the plates, he reached into the box and picked something out of the bottom.

"Hey, guys," he said. "Look at this."

"Shut up, Joe," said Max. "We're not talking to you."

"No, I'm serious," said Joe. "Look. I found this in the bottom of the box. It must have been hidden under that copper plate." He placed a grubby disc down on the table.

Charlie glanced at it and curled her lip. "It's a five-pence piece. So what?"

"It's a coin but it's not a five-pence piece," said Joe. "Take a proper look."

Max picked up the coin and held it to the light. The disc was a pale yellow color and it looked crudely made. On one side, a picture of a cross was stamped into the metal and on the other was a man's head, wearing a strange headdress. Max frowned. "This looks really old," he said. He rubbed the coin with his thumb. "And this metal looks like it might be...*gold!*"

Joe thumped his fist into his palm. "I knew it!" he cried. "It *is* Ragnar's Gold! We've found it."

"What we've found," said Charlie, "is one coin. There's no proof that this is part of Ragnar's Gold."

"It must be genuine," said Joe excitedly. "Otherwise, why would Cecilia Ufford have gone to so much trouble to hide it? She was on the trail of Ragnar's Gold. We have to ask Miss Pollock what she knows about her."

"You're forgetting we're going home first thing in the morning," said Lucy.

Joe groaned and rolled his eyes. "Come on, Lucy," he said. "How can we go home after all the things we've discovered tonight? We have to stay and find out more."

Max glanced guiltily at Lucy. "He's got a point, Luce," he said. "I mean, this could be a really important discovery. Let's investigate a little bit longer."

"Well, you've changed your tune," said Lucy. "A minute ago you were worried your mom wouldn't trust you. What do you think, Charlie?"

Charlie bit her lip and then shrugged. "Sorry, Lucy, I agree with Max and Joe. This is far more exciting than anything that's happening in Southwold. And if we're going to get into trouble for being here, then what difference will it make if we stay a bit longer?"

Lucy frowned. If she was honest, she was also excited by the prospect of Viking gold. She sat back in her seat and let out a huge sigh.

"All right," she said eventually. "We'll stay for one more day and do some investigating. But if we haven't solved the mystery by tomorrow, we're definitely going home. Agreed?"

"Agreed!" said Max, Joe, and Charlie all at the same time. Then they laughed out loud, because, however much trouble they might be about to get into, the prospect of finding lost treasure made it too exciting to worry about.

9

THE OLD CHAPEL

The following morning, Max woke early. For several seconds, he lay in bed looking up at the canopy of hanging drapes and wondered where on earth he was. Then it all came flooding back. He was in Ufford Castle and today they were going to look for Ragnar's Gold.

He pulled on a shirt, his second-best tie, and a pair of jeans, and descended the spiral stairs. In the Great Hall he found a bundle of bedclothes rolled up on the old sofa. The bundle stirred and Charlie poked her head out from beneath them, her eyes befuddled with sleep and her hair standing out at odd angles. A moment later,

Sherlock's head popped up beside her.

"What are you two doing down here?" asked Max.

"I just wanted a change, that's all," she mumbled, reaching for her sweatshirt.

"A change from what? You've got a luxury four-poster bed upstairs."

Charlie sighed. "If I tell you, do you promise not to tell Joe?"

Max sat in one of the squashy armchairs. "Er, sure," he said, puzzled. It was not like Charlie to worry about what Joe or anyone else thought of her.

Charlie sat up and hugged her knees. "I heard something in my room last night. There were strange noises coming from the chimney." She frowned, choosing her next words carefully. "Max, do you remember what Miss Pollock told us about King Edmund and Ragnar, and how people said they could still hear them doing battle underground?"

"Y-ees," said Max slowly.

"Well, do you think it's possible...I mean, do you think this castle might be *haunted*?"

Max opened his eyes wide in surprise. Charlie was the last person in the world he would have expected to ask him that question. "I don't believe in ghosts," he said.

"Yes, but weren't you the one who said you saw Black Shuck in the forest yesterday?"

Max squirmed uncomfortably. "I suppose I was," he said.

Charlie stared at him intently. "There's something very strange going on here, Max," she said.

At that moment, Joe came thundering down the stairs, having another imaginary sword fight. He was followed by Lucy, still yawning and scratching her head. "What's all the noise?" she demanded. "Do you have any idea how early it is?"

"I just thought we should get an early start," said Charlie, giving Max a warning look.

"Well, I don't think we'll be going anywhere in this," said Joe, looking out of the window.

Torrential rain lashed against the glass and the trees strained against the wind. "Let's have some breakfast. It will probably be sunny in half an hour."

But by the time they had finished breakfast, the wind and the rain were as bad as ever and they were forced to spend most of the morning waiting for the weather to clear. Joe and Lucy played cards while Charlie tried to teach Sherlock to sit up and woof for a treat.

Max spent the time examining the spidery writing in the old black notebook and looking up individual words in his Latin dictionary. "Have you figured out what it means, yet?" asked Lucy.

Max frowned. "Not really," he said. "It definitely says something about Viking gold. But it also says something about this only being half of the story. If it's a clue, then I don't think it's complete."

"Well, the rain's clearing up a bit," said Joe, looking out of the window again. "Let's go out. I think I'll climb the walls if I have to spend any longer in here."

They left the castle by the front entrance and waited while Joe used the iron key to secure the door behind them. The rain had stopped but they still had to lean into the wind as they walked. Lucy's ankle was hurting so they walked slowly, all except for Max, who had insisted on bringing his electric skateboard, which he had fitted with fat wheels that crunched along the gravel when he moved. Sherlock spent his time snuffling through the long grass and stopping at every tree to investigate all the exciting smells he never encountered in Southwold.

They had not gone far when they saw a tall figure coming toward them on horseback. "It's Miss Pollock," said Lucy. "And look at that horse!"

Miss Pollock was seated on a tall chestnut horse with a black mane and a well-groomed tail. She looked comfortable and secure, as though she had spent her entire life riding horses.

"Good afternoon," said Miss Pollock, as she pulled up the horse. "Did you have a good evening at the castle?" She frowned at Max's skateboard as though she disapproved of any form of transport that didn't have legs.

"Very good, thank you, Miss Pollock," said Lucy. "Your horse is so beautiful."

"This is Captain," said Miss Pollock. "You can pet him if you like. He's very well behaved."

They took turns rubbing Captain gently on the nose while the horse snorted and nodded his great head.

"We were wondering, Miss Pollock," said Max, "if you'd ever heard of a person named Cecilia Ufford? I read something about her in a history of the castle."

"Cecilia Ufford?" said Miss Pollock. "Yes, I know a little about her. She was the great-granddaughter of the fourteenth Earl of Ufford. Quite mad, so they say."

"Mad?" repeated Joe.

"Apparently she was convinced that the castle was cursed and that the curse could only be lifted if Ragnar's Gold was found and returned to its rightful owners. She spent most of her family's fortune searching for the treasure. She even hired a group of miners to dig up different parts of the castle grounds, but sadly she died before they ever found anything."

"What happened to her?" asked Joe.

"The poor girl drowned," said Miss Pollock. "In the very lake you swam in yesterday."

"Drowned?" said Lucy. She recoiled in shock. The thought of swimming in the same lake that someone had drowned in made her feel cold all over, even if it had been a very long time ago. "That's awful."

Miss Pollock nodded. "Some say she killed herself in despair when she couldn't find the gold. Others said it was Ragnar's curse. But it was probably nothing more than a tragic accident."

"Do you know anything else about her?" asked Max. "Did she ever say where she thought the gold was?"

"Not as far as I know," said Miss Pollock. "She's buried over there in the churchyard," she said, pointing through the trees. "You might find something about her in the parish records. Now, if you'll excuse me, I must get on. Captain gets very skittish if he doesn't get his daily exercise." She kicked her heels and Captain trotted off along the path. "Keep on the path until you get to the churchyard," she called out. "You can't miss it."

"We will," said Lucy as they all waved. "And thank you!"

They found the old churchyard just as Miss Pollock had described, a tiny stone chapel standing alone in a forest clearing. It was a plain structure with arched windows and a low porchway on the side. The stones of the old building were grimy and cracked and the gate to the churchyard hung half off its hinges.

All around the church stood ancient gravestones, green with moss and sticking out of the long grass

like crooked teeth. Some of the larger graves had elaborate marble crosses and thick marble pillars.

"Cheerful place," said Joe, pulling his jacket tighter. "Remind me what we're doing here?"

"Looking for information about Cecilia Ufford," said Max. "Let's start by finding her grave. It might give us some clues."

They spread out among the gravestones and

began to examine each one in turn. Max shivered as they worked. It was a chilly day and something about the graveyard made it feel like the cold was clinging to him, like a living thing. A faint mist hugged the ground and several large crows watched him from the trees. He looked around anxiously and realized he had lost sight of the others.

"Found anything yet?" he called out. He tried to make it sound like a casual inquiry, but his voice came out all high-pitched and squeaky.

Lucy's head popped up from behind a gravestone. "Not so far," she said. "Although nearly everyone here seems to have been named Ufford. There must be several generations buried in this graveyard."

Joe peered out from behind a stone angel. "Just imagine, after dark this place is probably filled with hundreds of dead Uffords, walking around like zombies." He assumed a blank expression and began to stagger around with his hands held out in front of him.

Max frowned. "Totally not funny, Joe."

"Over here!" called out Charlie. "I think I've got it."

They found Charlie and Sherlock at the edge of the graveyard where the graves were badly overgrown and clearly hadn't been looked after for a long while. At the end of the last row, Charlie had found a small gravestone, green with moss.

"*Cecilia Ufford*," read Max. "*Born 1734—Died 1763 —Cursed by madness.*"

"Well, that's cheerful," said Charlie.

"Miss Pollock said the poor girl drowned in the lake," said Lucy. "It sounds like she had a very sad life."

Joe looked up suddenly. "Shh!" he said.

"Everybody be quiet. I heard something, over there in the trees."

"Cut out the graveyard jokes, Joe," said Max. "It wasn't funny the first time."

"Wait," said Charlie. "Sherlock heard it too."

While they had been talking, the little dog had fixed his gaze on a patch of deep shadow. His ears had flattened and the hackles had risen on the back of his neck. "What's wrong with him?" asked Max in a small voice. He felt the same creeping sensation of being watched that he had felt yesterday. He was sure there was something just out of sight in the bushes.

As they watched, there was a sudden movement and a rustle of branches as something moved into deeper shadow. Sherlock began to bark and Charlie had to grab his collar to stop him from bolting.

"W-what was that?" said Joe.

"It must be the same thing I saw yesterday," blurted Max. "It's Black Shuck!"

A deep growl came from shadows, a noise

that could only have been made by a very large animal. Sherlock stopped barking and let out a small whine, and they all instinctively took a step backward.

"Okay, this is officially scary now," said Charlie. "What *is* that thing?"

There was a gleam in the shadows as a pair of eyes flashed, yellow and ringed with red fire. "Black Shuck!" shrieked Max. "I told you! Run for it!"

They ran as though their lives depended on it, snagging brambles and tripping over roots. Even Lucy managed to limp along at an impressive speed, using her stick for support, but eventually she stopped and grasped her ankle. "I can't run any farther," she said, wincing in pain.

Joe looked around. "Quick, everybody inside the church," he said. "We can take shelter in there."

They stumbled into the stone porch and Joe threw his weight against the solid oak door, which swung open with a creak. As they tumbled inside, Max looked back over his shoulder and felt sure he saw a shadow darting through the long grass toward them.

The moment they were inside, Joe slammed the door shut and they pressed their backs against it. They stood like that for several seconds, gasping for breath, their ears straining for any noises from outside. Max thought his heart might explode.

"W-was that it?" said Charlie, breaking the silence. "Was that the thing you saw in the bushes yesterday?"

Max swallowed. "I didn't get a good look at it," he said. "But I think so, yes. Maybe you guys will believe me now?"

When it was obvious that nothing was going to follow them inside, they began to take in their surroundings. The old chapel was tiny and simply constructed. A stained-glass window cast a warm glow over whitewashed stone walls. A dozen rows of polished pews faced the altar and a heavy marble font stood near the back of the church. The air smelled of candle wax and wood polish.

"It's lovely and peaceful in here," said Lucy, trying not to think too hard about the thing that had chased them inside.

"Well, get used to it," said Max. "We may have to stay in here until Black Shuck decides to go and eat some different kids."

"You don't think there really is such a thing as a demon-dog, do you?" asked Charlie. She kept a tight hold of Sherlock's collar as she spoke. Although the apparition had scared her, she had been most afraid for Sherlock, who she thought might try to fight the beast.

"Of course there isn't, stupid," said Joe. He seemed to have shaken off his earlier panic and was now behaving as though there had been nothing to worry about. "Max just got spooked, that's all."

"*I* got spooked?" said Max indignantly. "You were running faster than I was."

"Keep it down, everyone," said Lucy. "Remember we're in a church."

129

"How will we know when it's safe to go outside again?" asked Charlie.

"Well, I'm not going out to check," said Max. "I'm allergic to being eaten."

"Maybe there's a telephone we can use to call for help," said Lucy.

"If you ask me," said Joe, "you're all making a big fuss over nothing."

A door opened at the far end of the chapel and a voice called out, "Hello there? Can I help you?"

Joe let out a surprised shriek and they all turned to see a large woman emerging from a vestibule to one side of the altar. The woman had a cheerful round face with rosy cheeks, framed with graying hair. She smiled at them pleasantly and her eyes twinkled behind a pair of thick, black-rimmed glasses. She wore a threadbare gray suit and a black shirt with a white dog collar that indicated she was a vicar.

"Hello, my dears," she hailed them as she came up the aisle. "I'm terribly sorry but we're closed to visitors at the moment." She clasped her hands together in the way that only vicars do and gave them a beaming smile. "We're having a few restorations done, see?" She pointed to a heap of workman's tools and dust sheets sitting in a corner. "The old place is getting on a bit and takes some looking after. Just like me," she added.

She gave a horsey laugh at her own joke, rocking back and forth and screwing up her eyes with such obvious glee that the children couldn't help smiling along with her. "Don't pay me any attention," she gasped, taking off her glasses and wiping her eyes. "I swear my jokes get worse every year. Now, what can I do for you, my dears?"

"We're sorry to disturb you," said Lucy. "But we came in here to, er...research some local history. We thought you might be able to help us." Lucy thought it was probably best not to mention the demon-dog that had chased them in from the graveyard.

"Local history, is it?" said the vicar. "Well, I'll

certainly help if I can. Don't stand there in the doorway, come in, come in." She bustled about, moving dust sheets from the pews and then invited them to sit down. "So, where did you all come from exactly?"

"We're staying up at the castle," said Max. "I'm Max, this is Lucy, Joe, and Charlie, and that's Sherlock."

"Well, I'm delighted to meet such a charming group of young people," she said. "I'm the Reverend Harriet Graves. I'm the local vicar here. So, tell me, what is it you'd like to know?"

"We're trying to find out something about Cecilia Ufford, who lived in the castle two hundred and fifty years ago," said Max. "Miss Pollock said there might be some records about her here."

The Reverend Graves frowned. "Two hundred and fifty years ago?" she said, scratching her head. "Well, that's a little before my time, I'm afraid. I don't think I can help you there."

"Could we have a look at the parish records?"

said Lucy. "We promise we won't get in the way of your workmen."

"Ordinarily that wouldn't be a problem, my dear," said the Reverend Graves. "But I'm afraid all of our parish records are being stored at the town hall for safekeeping while the work is done." She shrugged apologetically and then brightened again. "Perhaps you'd like a ticket for the church fete instead?" she said. "We're having a raffle and the first prize is one of Mrs. Dewsbury's Battenberg cakes."

Lucy shook her head. "Sorry, but I don't think we'll be staying that long."

Reverend Graves looked disappointed. "I understand," she said. Then she glanced over her shoulder and lowered her voice. "It's probably for the best anyway. Mrs. Dewsbury is the worst cook in the parish. Her Battenberg cake tastes like soggy cardboard." She brayed with laughter again then slapped her knees and stood up abruptly. "Well, I'm really sorry I couldn't be any more help, my dears. But if there's anything—"

"Have you ever heard of the legend of Black Shuck?" said Max suddenly. "We heard he roams around these parts." Max was not quite sure why he had asked the question right at that moment but the effect on the vicar was immediate.

The Reverend Graves placed her hand on her heart and gave an audible gasp. Then she sat back down. "Oh my," she said.

"Are you all right?" said Lucy, concerned.

The vicar took a deep breath and blew out slowly. "Yes, yes, I'm fine, thank you, my dear," she said, patting Lucy's hand. "You just took me by surprise, that's all. What makes you ask about Black Shuck?"

"We saw him in your churchyard, just now," said Joe. "That's why we came in here to take shelter."

The vicar's eyes opened wide and she gripped the edge of the pew. "Oh my," she said again. "You saw Black Shuck, *here*? In *my* churchyard?" She turned very pale.

"Is there something wrong?" asked Lucy. "You don't look very well."

The vicar took another deep breath, then gave them a weak smile. "I'm sorry," she said. "But you gave me a bit of a shock when you mentioned Black Shuck. You see, when I first came to this parish, I'd heard tales about the demon-hound, but I never paid any attention to that sort of nonsense. But there have been nights here when I felt sure there was something watching me from the forest."

"Watching you?" said Joe.

The vicar nodded gravely. "Several times I've felt its presence," she said. "And once I swear I saw a pair of red and yellow eyes looking at me from the darkness, like the eyes of the devil." She shivered. "I'm not the sort of person who scares easily, my dears," she said. "But I'm certain that Black Shuck is more than just a legend. There's something evil roaming in this forest, you mark my words."

She stopped talking and a chill silence descended over the old church. Lucy couldn't help noticing how dark it had become outside. "Well, I really wouldn't worry too much," she said. "We probably just saw a deer or something. I should imagine it's gone by now."

The vicar swallowed and nodded. "Yes, yes, maybe you're right," she said. She looked up at the window and the fading light outside. "But you should probably go now. Best to get back to the castle before it gets dark."

Without waiting for an answer, she went to the church door and peered out. The children gathered behind her and looked over her shoulder. A deep gloom had settled over the forest, which seemed unnaturally still. Barely a leaf stirred in the trees. "It certainly seems pretty quiet," said Joe.

"I think the coast is clear now," said Reverend Graves. "Now, I'd suggest going home as quickly as possible, while there's still some light left. And, whatever you do, don't return to the forest after dark. They say that's when Black Shuck comes looking for souls to claim."

All the children felt a cold shiver at her words. "Will you be all right, Reverend Graves?" said Lucy. "Aren't you worried about Black Shuck?"

The vicar gave a brave smile. "Don't worry about me," she said. "I won't stay here any longer than I have to." She gave another glance around the graveyard. "But I'll be happier when I know you're all safely back at the castle. Now go!"

Before they could argue, the Reverend Harriet Graves ushered them outside. She gave them another brave smile and watched from the doorway while they walked down the path. Then she shut the heavy oak doors and they heard the sound of several bolts being driven home.

"Well," said Joe. "How do you like that?"

"She seemed all right until we mentioned Black Shuck," said Max. "Then she looked scared half to death."

Lucy glanced around the empty graveyard and shivered. "Well, if we really did see Black Shuck, he seems to be gone now. But the Reverend Graves was right about one thing. It *is* getting dark so I suggest we do what she says and get out of this forest as quickly as possible."

They all agreed that was an excellent idea and none of them wanted to spend any longer there than they had to. They had already started back down the forest track when Max stopped suddenly. "Everybody, wait up," he said. "I left my skateboard behind. I must have dropped it when we started running."

"Well, go back and get it quick," said Joe. "We'll wait here."

Max had hoped the others would offer to come with him, but they didn't, so he returned to the churchyard alone. Looking around anxiously, he found his skateboard where he had dropped it, right next to Cecilia Ufford's grave. He was about to leave again when he noticed there was a strange design etched on the back of the gravestone that he hadn't seen before. It was a series of scratchy lines, criss-crossing the back of the stone.

They made no sense to him, and yet, they looked very much like something else he had seen recently.

He quickly pulled his phone from his pocket and took a picture of the gravestone. Then he picked up his skateboard and ran back to join the others. He wasn't sure what it all meant yet, but he had a hunch. And if he was correct, then this discovery might just unlock the secret of Ragnar's Gold.

10

STEGANOGRAPHY

The children hurried back to the castle, anxiously looking over their shoulders for any sign of the black beast they had seen in the graveyard. But nothing followed them through the forest or watched them from the shadows. It was as if the specter of Black Shuck had just disappeared, like smoke on the breeze.

Thick clouds covered the sky and even though it was still afternoon, the light was fading fast. When they reached the castle, Joe fumbled with the keys and they hurried inside, then headed straight downstairs to the kitchen.

"I need something to eat," said Max, sitting

down at the large table. "Nearly getting mauled by a demon-dog always makes me hungry."

"Is there anything that doesn't make you hungry?" asked Lucy.

Max thought for a moment. "Eating?" he offered.

"How about I make you my specialty dish," said Joe. "*Haricots cuits, avec du jus de tomate, sur du pain grillé.*" Joe spoke with a surprisingly good French accent and the others stared at him blankly.

"Which would be what?" asked Lucy.

"Beans on toast," said Joe, grinning.

"Sounds perfect," said Max. "And a large mug of tea with four sugars, please."

While Joe opened the baked beans, Charlie fed Sherlock and then set to work building a fire in the kitchen fireplace. There was a basket of firewood beside the hearth. She placed some old newspaper, kindling, and a few dry logs into the grate and held a lighted match to it. Moments later, the flames were licking around the logs and the kitchen was bathed in a warm glow.

"That's more like it," said Max, holding out his hands to the fire. "I could get used to this." He leaned back in his chair and took out his phone, frowning with concentration as he peered at the screen.

Lucy raised an eyebrow. "Any time you feel like doing something useful, Max," she said as she placed the bread in the toaster. "There's plenty to do over here."

"I'll have you know I *am* doing something useful," said Max. "I'm thinking about the clues we found on our visit to the graveyard."

"We didn't find any clues," said Joe. "Not unless you count a lady vicar and a phantom dog."

"That's where you're wrong," said Max. "Look at this picture I took of Cecilia Ufford's grave." He held up his phone and the others crowded around to look at the strange markings Max had discovered on the back of the gravestone.

"They're just scratches," said Joe. "They don't mean anything."

"They look familiar, though," said Lucy. "I've seen them somewhere before."

"They're like the scratches we found on the copper plate," said Charlie. "I think they're the same."

"Not quite the same," said Max. He took the copper sheet from the box and placed it beside his phone so they could be compared side by side.

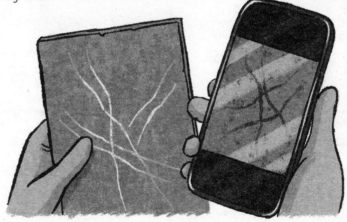

"They *are* different," said Joe. "But they still don't mean anything."

"I think they do," said Max. "Have you ever heard of something called "steganography"?

"Does it have something to do with dinosaurs?" asked Joe.

"It has nothing to do with dinosaurs, Joe," said Max. "Steganography is the art of hiding things in plain sight. I read a book about it once. A long time ago when people wanted to send a secret message, they'd sometimes put it in a place that was easy to see but which no one would ever notice. Like hidden in the details of a painting or the pattern in a carpet."

"Or on the back of a gravestone!" said Lucy.

"Exactly," said Max. "I think the message on Cecilia Ufford's gravestone has been hidden in plain sight for the last two hundred and fifty years."

Charlie looked at the picture. "Well, I still can't see any message," she said. "It just looks like a lot of scratches to me."

"That's because it's not complete," said Max. He picked up the copper sheet. "Do you remember what the inscription in Cecilia Ufford's notebook said about this only being half the message?

Well, what if the scratches on the back of her gravestone are the other half?"

Lucy blinked. "Are you saying that if we put these two pictures together, it might somehow lead us to Ragnar's Gold?"

"I think so, yes," said Max.

"Put them together how?" asked Charlie.

"I've got an idea," said Max. "Watch this."

They looked over his shoulder as Max opened an app on his phone for editing photographs. First, he loaded the picture of the gravestone and placed it in the center of the screen. Then he loaded the picture he had taken of the copper plate and laid it on top of the first one. He adjusted the settings on the screen and, very slowly, the pictures became slightly transparent, so that they could see the two images laid one on top of the other.

"They fit together!" gasped Lucy. "It's one picture that's been split into two."

Max nodded and grinned. When the two

pictures were laid on top of one another, the random scratches became a joined-up network of lines. The image suddenly made sense.

"It's a map!" said Joe breathlessly. "Cecilia Ufford drew a map and hid one half on this copper sheet and then had the other half placed on her own gravestone."

"But a map of what?" asked Lucy.

"It's obvious, isn't it?" said Charlie suddenly. "Miss Pollock told us that Cecilia Ufford had hired miners to dig all over the grounds, looking for Ragnar's Gold. I'm betting it's a map of the tunnels they made."

They looked at the image on Max's phone again. "I think Charlie's right," said Max. "And look, this mark here looks like it might be a tower, and this one over here looks like a cross. I bet that's the castle and that's the chapel. It looks like these tunnels go right underneath the castle grounds almost as far as the old burial mound."

"Well, I don't see how this is going to help us,"

said Joe. "Cecilia Ufford never found anything, did she? What use is a treasure map that doesn't lead to treasure?"

"Maybe she did find something," said Charlie. She pointed to another spot on the map. "Look at this mark here. It looks like the letter V. What could that mean?"

"Maybe it stands for Viking!" said Max. "What if Cecilia Ufford really did find the Viking treasure after all? Maybe that's the place where it's buried."

"Max, that's amazing!" said Lucy.

Max leaned back in his chair, breathed on his fingernails, then polished them on his lapel. "Oh, it was nothing," he said. "Anyone with the IQ of a genius could have figured it out."

"Okay then, genius," said Charlie. "If these really are tunnels, then how do we get into them?"

Max frowned. "I'm not sure," he said. He ran a finger over the image. "But a lot of these lines seem to converge on the castle. There must be an entrance somewhere around here."

"What about down in the dungeons?" suggested Joe. "That's the obvious place to put a secret passage."

"There aren't any dungeons here," said Max. "At least none that we've seen."

"Behind the walls, then?" said Joe. "Maybe if we went around the castle tapping on the wood paneling, we might find a hidden door?"

"That would take forever," said Max. "We have to face it, there's nothing around here that looks like the entrance to a tunnel."

"Yes, there is," said Charlie. "What about the well that Sherlock fell down yesterday? There was a ladder running down the inside of it. What if it isn't a well at all? What if that's the entrance to Cecilia Ufford's tunnels?"

"Charlie, you're brilliant!" said Max. "Of course! It's the only place the tunnels could start around here. That's where we should look."

"Wait," said Lucy. "There's something you're all forgetting. We agreed we were going to go home after today. We don't actually have permission to be here, remember?"

The others all groaned. "But we *can't* go home now, Lucy," said Joe. "Not when we're so close to finding Ragnar's Gold."

"Joe's right," said Max. "Now that we've found the secret map, who knows where it might lead? I couldn't bear to go home now."

"Besides," said Charlie, "we could investigate the tunnels tonight and still go home in the morning if we don't find anything."

Lucy drew a deep breath. Surely, it wouldn't hurt to stay a little longer? Just to see if Max was right about the tunnels? "All right," she said. "I suppose it won't do any harm to have a little look tonight. But we absolutely have to go home first thing in the morning."

The others cheered loudly and Joe and Max began to dance around the kitchen chanting "Rag-nar's Gold! Rag-nar's Gold!" over and over again until Sherlock began to howl in sympathy and Lucy couldn't help laughing. "That's enough!" she said. "If we're going to find these tunnels, let's get going."

Max stopped dancing and looked serious. "Okay, but before we go hunting for Viking gold, there's something really important we should do first."

"What's that?" asked Lucy.

"Let's eat Joe's *haricots cuits, avec du jus de tomate, sur du pain grillé,*" he said with a grin. "I'm starving."

11

THE PLAN

They ate their beans on toast in record time, then dumped the plates in the sink before heading up the back stairs. Joe paused to retrieve a flashlight from the cupboard, and they went outside.

They worked their way around the tower to the deep hole that Sherlock had fallen into the night before. With the wooden cover gone, the hole yawned, black and forbidding. Joe shone his flashlight down the shaft and the beam illuminated the brickwork for ten yards or so before it was absorbed by the darkness.

"How far down do you suppose it goes?" asked Charlie.

"Let's find out," said Joe. He picked up a small stone and dropped it into the hole. They all listened until they heard the distant clatter as the stone hit the bottom.

"It fell for about two seconds," said Joe. "That means the depth must be about...er..."

"Six and a half feet," said Max at once. The others stared at him in amazement. "What?" he said defensively. "It's just a simple equation."

"You really are a geek, aren't you?" said Charlie.

"Okay," said Joe. "It's time to investigate. Stand back, everyone." Gripping the flashlight in his teeth, Joe clambered over the side of the hole and began to let himself down on the iron rungs, just as Charlie had done the night before.

The others watched him go, the beam from the flashlight forming a ring of light on the brickwork as he went down. He passed the spot where Sherlock had been trapped and continued on into the darkness, the light getting fainter as he went. Then the light stopped moving.

"Joe, are you okay?" called Lucy. Her words echoed around the brickwork. "Can you hear us?"

"I'm all right." Joe's voice sounded hollow and distant. "It's definitely not a well. It's dry down here." They saw his light moving around in the bottom of the hole and then he yelled out, "I've found it!"

They craned over the edge of the hole and even Sherlock squeezed his way in between Lucy and Charlie for a look. "What is it?" shouted Max. "What have you found?"

"A tunnel," shouted Joe. "It looks like it goes right underneath the castle. We were right, this is definitely the way in."

A moment later, Joe's light disappeared completely, leaving the hole in total darkness. The others looked nervously at each other. "Joe!" shouted Lucy. "Are you okay? Speak to us!"

There was silence from the hole. "Joe!" yelled Max. "If this is one of your jokes, it really isn't funny."

"What if he's hurt himself?" asked Charlie.

Lucy sighed. "We should never have let Joe go down there first," she said. "We should have known that you can't trust him to—"

The light reappeared.

"I'm okay!" came Joe's voice. "I just went along the tunnel a little way. Hang on a minute, I'm coming back up."

There was a short pause, and then the light began to move steadily back up the shaft. After a while they could hear Joe puffing and panting as he climbed the last few rungs. When he reached the top, his eyes were shining.

"We were right," he said excitedly as he climbed out

of the hole. "There's a tunnel that leads under the castle. It's big enough to stand up in. Come on, let's all go and take a look."

"Wait a minute," said Charlie. "What about Sherlock? He can't climb down ladders and I can't leave him up here on his own."

"We could lower him down on the rope we used last night," said Max. "It's still in the cupboard back at the castle."

"Good idea," said Lucy. "We should get some more flashlights too. And we should bring some food and something to drink."

They returned to the castle, moving as quickly as Lucy's ankle would allow. Back in the kitchen they set about collecting the things they would need. Joe found more flashlights in the cupboard together with some spare batteries so that they could have a flashlight each. Charlie fetched the rope from the cupboard and also found an old-fashioned wicker shopping basket with a handle.

"We can tie the rope to this," she said. "It will be

a lot more comfortable for Sherlock to ride down in the basket."

Max packed a backpack with some bottled water and a handful of Lucy's protein bars "in case of emergencies." Lastly, he sat down at the kitchen table and consulted his phone while he sketched something on a sheet of paper.

"What are you doing?" asked Lucy. She was sitting on the kitchen floor, strapping her ankle with an extra-tight bandage so she would be able to climb down the ladder. It had been hurting her a lot but she was not going to miss their adventure in the tunnels for anything.

"I'm copying the map onto this sheet of paper so that if we run into any problems, people will know where to come and look for us," said Max. "And I'll send you all a copy in case we get separated down there."

"Good thinking," said Lucy, tying off the bandage. "All right, if we've got everything we need, let's get going."

"Wait a minute," said Joe. "What's that noise?"

They raised their eyes toward the ceiling, where a faint trilling sound was coming from the floor above. "It sounds like a fire alarm," said Lucy.

"It's not a fire alarm," said Charlie. "It's a telephone bell. It's coming from upstairs."

They found the telephone in the Great Hall, on the wall beside one of the windows. It was an old-fashioned model with a brass dial and a mouthpiece and a separate part, shaped like a trumpet, that you had to hold to your ear. It was ringing with a sharp, insistent jangle that grated on the nerves.

"Aren't you going to answer it?" said Charlie, looking at Joe.

Joe stepped back. "Why me?" he said. "It's not my phone."

"Because you were the one who brought us here," said Lucy. "It's more likely to be for you than anyone else."

Joe looked unsure. "But who do you think it is?"

"Here's a crazy idea," said Charlie. "How about you *answer* the thing and find out? And do it quickly, that noise is driving me nuts."

Joe gulped and stepped up to the phone. He picked up the earpiece and held it to his ear. "Hello?"

"Joseph Carter! How *dare* you go and stay in that castle without telling us!" The voice on the other end was loud and *very* angry.

Joe's heart sank. "Oh, hi, Mom," he said.

"Don't you "hi, Mom" me!" shouted Penelope Carter. "I've been going out of my mind with worry, young man. I spent all last night trying to call you at home and got no answer. This morning I telephoned your friends' parents and I learned that you'd all 'gone off to stay in a castle' for the week. I've never been so embarrassed in my *life*."

"Don't worry, Mom," said Joe weakly. "It's absolutely fine."

"It is *not* absolutely fine!" His mother was now yelling so loudly that he had to hold the earpiece away from his ear. "When I finally got hold of your grandmother, she told me all about the message you were supposed to give me. You *lied* to us, Joseph!"

"Weeell...it wasn't *exactly* a lie," said Joe. "I mean, technically I didn't say anything that wasn't true. I just—"

"Be quiet, Joseph," said his mother. "You've wrecked my vacation with the Santorinis. This was my chance to make an impression on some of the biggest names in fashion and it's ruined. *Ruined!*"

"You can still have your vacation," said Joe desperately. "We'll be okay here for a few more days. We've got everything we need and—"

"That's *enough!*" shouted Penelope. Joe bit his lip. His mom had not been this angry with him since he took the family motorboat without permission at Christmas. "Your father is already on his way back to England," she continued. "He insisted on catching the first flight back from the airport."

Penelope let out a choking sob. "I'm too angry to speak to you now, Joseph," she said. "Your father will get to the castle first thing in the morning and you had better be ready when he arrives."

The line went suddenly dead. Joe looked at the receiver in shock. His heart was hammering like a steam piston and his mouth had gone completely dry. When he turned to the others, they were all staring at him.

"Well," he said, as he replaced the receiver. "I think we're busted."

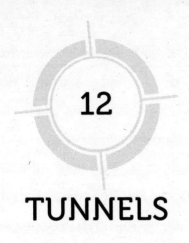

12

TUNNELS

They sat around the kitchen table, staring gloomily into space. Sherlock looked up at the children with a puzzled expression. He would never understand humans. One moment they were buzzing with excitement and the next they looked as though they had lost their favorite bone. He settled down in front of the fire and rested his head on his paws.

"I can't believe we were so close," said Max. "A few more hours and we might have found Ragnar's Gold. I'm going to be in so much trouble this time. I'll be doing extra math homework until I retire."

"It's not that bad," said Joe. "After all, you guys didn't really do anything wrong. I was the one that lied. If your mom's going to blame someone, she can blame me."

"Oh, she will, Joe," said Max. "Believe me, she's already convinced that you're part of a criminal conspiracy to bring down my grades. She'll be driving you away with garlic and holy water after this."

"Well, it was fun while it lasted," said Charlie.

"If only we'd had time to explore the tunnels," said Joe.

"We still *have* time," said Lucy suddenly. "If we want to, that is." They all turned to look at her. Since the phone call, Lucy had been very thoughtful. Now she was looking at them with a serious expression.

"In case you haven't kept up with current events," said Joe, "we're busted. My dad's on his way back to England and he'll be here in the morning."

"Exactly," said Lucy. "He'll be here in the morning. Which is a whole..." She checked her watch. "...twelve hours away. That's plenty of time to do some exploring, wouldn't you say?"

"You're joking, aren't you?" said Joe. "When I get home my folks are going to shut me in my room and brick up the doorway."

"Then what have you got to lose?" said Lucy. "If we're already in trouble, it won't make much difference if we spend all night exploring the tunnels. We might even have another adventure along the way."

"Lucy's right," said Charlie. "We should go down to the tunnels like we planned. After all, how many different ways can your parents punish you for the same thing?"

"I don't know," said Max. "My mom can be pretty inventive when it comes to punishments."

But something about Lucy's words had stirred excitement in Max's chest. Much as he wasn't looking forward to facing his mom, the thought of never having explored the tunnels was too awful to think about. "All right," he said after a few moments. "I'm in."

Joe grinned. "All right then, me too," he said. "Even if we don't find anything, we'll still have the best stories to tell when we get back to school."

"Wow, Lucy," said Max. "You were the last person in the world I would have expected to make that suggestion. You're always so...*sensible.*"

Lucy smiled. "I guess even sensible people have to do something daring occasionally. Come on then, let's get going. We've only got eleven hours and fifty-eight minutes left."

There was a frantic flurry of activity as they rushed around, gathering up bags, baskets, ropes, and flashlights. Sherlock was immediately awake and rushing around the kitchen too in a state of high excitement. The little dog had no idea why the children were suddenly happy again; he was just glad that they were going somewhere. He would never understand humans, he thought.

It was properly dark outside now and the full moon had risen, giving them enough light to find their way without the flashlights. When they reached the brick-lined shaft, Joe shone his flashlight into the hole.

"I'll go first," he said. "Then the three of you can lower Sherlock down in the basket and I'll take him out at the bottom." They agreed this was a good idea and watched as Joe descended the tunnel again, disappearing into the gloom until they could just see his flashlight.

"Okay, I'm at the bottom," he called up. "Send down Sherlock next."

Charlie tied the rope firmly around the handle of the shopping basket, using several knots to make sure that her precious cargo would be safe on his journey. Then she lifted a slightly mystified Sherlock into the basket. "Now then, Sherlock, my love," said Charlie earnestly. "It's really important that you sit absolutely still for this. We can't have you jumping around while we're lowering you down."

A small frown wrinkled Sherlock's forehead. He had no idea what Charlie was saying but he recognized her serious tone of voice and knew he had to be on his best behavior. He sat very still in the basket as they lowered it over the side and bumped his way gently to the bottom.

"Okay, he's here," shouted Joe, a few moments later. "He's fine but he looks a little confused."

Charlie went down next, climbing confidently. She was followed, rather more slowly, by Max. Max had never been fond of heights and was trying hard not to think about how far it might be to the bottom of the shaft.

Last of all came Lucy. She took a deep breath before starting down the ladder. Her ankle was hurting her more than she'd been letting on, but somehow the excitement had made it feel less painful. She reached the bottom to find the others standing in a space slightly wider than the shaft. The walls were lined with brick and the air smelled cool, damp, and slightly earthy.

Sherlock began to bark when he saw Lucy coming down the ladder, and his bark echoed back a dozen times from the tunnel. The little dog promptly ducked behind Charlie's legs and sat down. He was not sure he liked this place.

To one side of them, an archway framed the entrance to a black tunnel. Joe's flashlight illuminated a brick passageway with a dry earth floor. "I went down there a little way," he said. "I think it goes right under the castle."

Max checked his phone and consulted the map. "According to this, the main tunnel runs south for a bit and then splits into two. The right-hand tunnel goes under the castle grounds and the left goes toward the churchyard. There are lots of side tunnels too. We should be careful not to get lost."

Lucy bent down and fetched a small piece of

chalky stone from the floor. She used the stone to draw an arrow on the wall. "We'll mark our path as we go," she said. "Every time we come to a junction we'll draw an arrow to show us the way back to the shaft."

They walked in single file with Joe leading, followed by Charlie and Sherlock, Max, and, finally, Lucy. "These tunnels are well built," said Max. His voice echoed alarmingly when he spoke. "Cecilia Ufford really went to town looking for this gold."

"Hey, look at that," said Charlie. She pointed to the tunnel floor just ahead of Joe. "Someone's been here before us."

They shone their flashlights on the ground and saw that it was true. The imprints of several heavy boots could be clearly seen in the dust. "Are they old footprints?" asked Joe.

"I don't think so," said Max. "I'm no expert but these look like fresh boot prints."

Lucy crouched down to examine the prints carefully. "It *does* look like someone has been down here recently," she said. "We should be careful. We're not supposed to be here ourselves, don't forget."

They continued until they reached the fork in the tunnel that Max had predicted. "All right!" he declared. "The map is accurate!

"But which tunnel should we take?" asked Joe.

"I vote we go toward the chapel," said Lucy.

Max shrugged. "Okay, it's as good a direction as any. You'd think Cecilia Ufford would have paid these miners to put up a few signposts."

Lucy marked the wall with another arrow and they took the left-hand passageway. The roof was lower here and the walls were not as well finished. In some places they were little more than soft earth and rock. Before long, the children were stiff and uncomfortable from having to bend their backs.

"How much longer, do you think?" gasped Lucy. "I'm not sure which is hurting more, my ankle or my neck."

"We're nearly there," said Max, looking at his

phone. "Though who knows how accurate the scale is on this map."

"Shh! There's a light up ahead," said Joe in a loud whisper. "Turn off the flashlights."

The flashlights went out and they peered ahead into the darkness. A soft light was coming from around a bend in the tunnel. There was no sound save for Sherlock scratching himself in the darkness.

"Everybody, go slowly," whispered Joe. "Follow me."

They crept forward until they reached the bend in the tunnel. Then they stopped and blinked.

"Holy cow!" said Joe. "Look at that."

The tunnel was filled with white light, which felt unbearably bright after the darkness. A thick electric cable was strung along the walls in loops and every few feet a glowing bulb hung down, protected by a small wire cage. The tunnel had been widened in several places and earth and rocks had been piled into rough spoil heaps.

Pickaxes and shovels leaned against the walls and there was a rickety table, piled with smaller tools, boxes, and reference books.

"You don't suppose," said Joe, after a pause, "that Cecilia's miners left all this behind, do you?"

"Electricity hadn't been invented in 1758," said Max scornfully. "All of this has been put here recently."

"Didn't the Reverend Graves say they were having some work done at the chapel?" said Lucy. "Perhaps this has something to do with that?"

"We're not in the chapel," said Max. "And this doesn't look like any ordinary sort of work."

"Sherlock, get away from there!" hissed Charlie. While they had been talking, Sherlock had started snuffling among a pile of boxes. He reached into a plastic bag on the floor and came out holding half a cheese sandwich in his jaws, looking very pleased with himself. "Put that down," said Charlie, taking it from his mouth. "You don't know where it's been."

Sherlock gave Charlie a hurt look as she took away his sandwich. He could never understand why she wouldn't let him eat perfectly good food when other people obviously didn't want it. But Charlie wasn't paying attention to Sherlock now. She was looking at the objects scattered across the table. She moved aside an old rag and gave a gasp. "Look at this!" she cried.

The others gathered around the table. Laid out on a piece of soft cloth were about a dozen rough-cut coins. They were a dirty yellow color with a cross stamped on one side and a man's head on the other.

"These are just like the coin we found in Cecilia's box!" said Max. "Whoever has been digging down here must have found them."

Some of the coins had been wrapped in plastic and others had been packed into small cardboard boxes. Lucy lifted one of the sealed boxes from the table and peered at the writing on the front of it. "These boxes are all addressed to people in different countries," she said.

"And look over there," said Joe, pointing along the tunnel. "There's a ladder. It must be another way out."

At the end of the tunnel, an aluminum ladder led up into a narrow shaft. When they shone their flashlights up into the hole, they could see a flat piece of white stone laid across the top of the shaft. Joe climbed the ladder and pressed his hands against the stone.

"It won't budge," he called down. "But there's a crack here." He pressed his eye against the edge of the stone. "I can see electric light, which means it must be inside a building," he cried. He shifted position and placed his other eye against the crack. "It's the chapel we were in earlier," he said. "I recognize the pews from here." He drew back and tapped on the white stone. "I bet this is the marble font, covering up the tunnel entrance. Do you suppose the Reverend Graves knows anything about this?"

"Probably not," said Lucy. "I don't think she would come poking around down here if she could help it. She seemed as scared of Black Shuck as we were."

At that moment, Sherlock began to growl. His ears went back on his head and he bared his teeth as he looked up at the hole. "Something's wrong," said Charlie. "I think Sherlock's heard someone."

Joe pressed his ear to the stone. "I can hear voices," he said in a whisper. "Two men. And it sounds like they're coming this way."

"Joe, get down from there!" hissed Lucy.

Joe slid back down the ladder and Charlie held Sherlock's collar as they all stared up at the shaft. They could hear the distant murmuring of voices from above. The sound drew closer and then stopped.

"They've gone quiet," whispered Max. "What do you think they're doing?"

Then came a noise that chilled them all to the core: the grinding sound of stone on stone. "Oh no!" said Joe. "They're sliding back the font. Quick, everyone, run!"

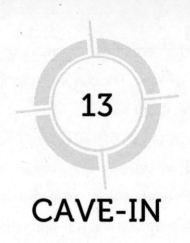

13

CAVE-IN

The white stone font slid back from the entrance in rough, jerky movements. They could hear puffing and grunting from above as someone struggled to move the heavy weight. "Everybody, get out of sight," hissed Lucy.

The four children backed away from the stone shaft as quietly as they could, but Sherlock had other ideas. As far as Sherlock was concerned, he had arrived in the tunnel first, and that meant it belonged to him. The moment a man's leg appeared through the hole and stood on the top of the ladder, he began to bark furiously.

"Sherlock, shut up," hissed Charlie. She dragged

him away by his collar, but the damage had already been done. The leg disappeared back up the hole.

"What's going on?" came a shout from above. "Who's down there?"

There was a whispered conversation at the top of the shaft followed by some scuffling. Then a very large man began to climb down the ladder. He had a thick black beard and wore heavy boots. His arms and body were muscular and his overalls bulged at the seams. When he saw the children, his eyes widened with astonishment.

"Who are you?" he boomed.

"What is it?" called the second voice. "Levi! What's going on down there?"

The big man scratched his head in a confused way. "There's a bunch of kids down here, Topper," he called out. "Four of 'em, plus a little dog." He looked warily at Sherlock, who was still straining against his collar.

"What do you mean, kids?" said the second voice.

"The boss is going to be here at any minute and I don't want to be the one that has to explain this. You know what a nasty temper the boss has." There was a clattering of boots and a second man came down the ladder.

The second man was as skinny as the first was large. He had a pinched face with a fuzz of ginger hair on top and ferrety eyes, which darted around the children.

"What are you doing down here?" he demanded. "Come on, spit it out!" The muscles of his face twitched uncontrollably when he spoke.

"W-we didn't mean any harm," stammered Max. "We're sorry to have bothered you."

"W-we were just leaving," said Joe.

"You've obviously got more important things to do," said Lucy.

The skinny man scowled and nudged his accomplice in the ribs. "Don't just stand there, Levi, you big ox! Grab them."

"Run!" yelled Charlie.

As Levi charged after them, the children bolted into the nearest tunnel and ran, following the light of Joe's flashlight and ducking their heads. They could hear Levi, lumbering through the narrow space behind them and swearing each time he struck his head on the low tunnel roof.

When they reached a fork in the tunnel, Joe chose one without hesitation and they plunged down it. They took another fork, then another, all the time wondering if they would run up against a dead end. In the end, it was Lucy who brought them to a stop.

"Everybody, please, wait!" she cried out from the back. They turned to see Lucy sitting on the floor of the tunnel, nursing her injured ankle. "I'm sorry, but I can't run any farther. My ankle is just too painful."

Joe glanced anxiously back along the tunnel but there was no sign that anyone was following. "It sounds like they've given up the chase," he said. "We can stop here for a bit."

"Where is *here*, exactly?" asked Charlie, leaning against the wall. "I don't recognize this tunnel at all."

Joe shone the flashlight around. "I have no idea," he said. "I wasn't really keeping track of which way we were going."

The tunnel was not brick-lined like the first one they had seen. It was made of rough earth and stone and propped up with old mine timbers. The wood looked black and ancient.

Max took out his phone and consulted his map. Then he sucked his teeth. "I think we're in this tunnel here," he said, expanding the image. "It's close to the letter V that Cecilia Ufford marked on the map, but it looks like it's a dead end. We'll have to go back the way we came."

They let out a collective groan. None of them particularly wanted to meet the two men again. "Let's take a break first," said Lucy. "I've got some crackers in my bag."

They all agreed and sat down with their backs to the damp wall while Lucy rummaged in her backpack. Sherlock had been looking back along the tunnel and growling softly, as though he expected the big man to come lumbering out of the darkness. But the moment he heard the rustle of the cracker wrappers, he stopped growling and positioned himself next to Lucy.

"What do you think those men were up to?" said Charlie, breaking a cracker into small pieces for her dog. "Sherlock didn't like them one bit."

"I don't think they were workmen," said Max. "They didn't seem to be repairing anything and it looks like they've been digging down here for some time."

"Do you think they're hunting for Ragnar's Gold too?" said Lucy.

Max nodded. "It looks like it," he said. "From all that equipment they have, I'd say they're serious treasure hunters. They must be coming down here at night after the Reverend Graves has gone home. I bet she has no idea that they're digging for treasure right underneath her chapel."

"You don't think they've already found it, do you?" said Joe, trying to keep the disappointment out of his voice.

"I don't think so," said Max. "They might have found some stray coins while they were digging, but there weren't a whole lot of them. I think they must be still trying to find the main part of the treasure."

Charlie snapped her fingers. "That explains the noises I heard in my bedroom," she said. "All that crashing and banging I heard was them digging. The sound must have carried through the stonework and up the chimney. That means the castle isn't haunted after all." A look of relief washed over her face.

"If they are looking for Ragnar's Gold, then why are they being so secretive about it?" asked Lucy. "After all, anyone is allowed look for treasure if they want to, aren't they?"

"Anyone can look if they have permission," said Joe. "But if you actually *find* treasure, you can't just keep it. If it's really valuable, then it belongs to the whole nation and it has to go to a museum."

"Well, that explains why they're doing it at night," said Max. "They didn't look like they were planning to hand anything over to the authorities. Those gold coins we saw were being sent abroad. I think they're planning to sell everything they find down here."

"We should tell the police," said Joe. "We might even get another bravery award."

"We won't be telling anyone unless we can find a way out of this maze," said Lucy. "That's the first thing we should do."

"Easier said than done," said Joe. "We could wander around in here for days until our food and water run out and we starve to death. Then in a hundred years' time they'll find our skeletons lying next to Ragnar's Gold, just like in the pirate movies."

"Good grief!" said Charlie. "Is your mouth *actually* connected to your brain or do they just work completely independently?"

"We're not going to starve to death, Joe," said Lucy. "I'm more worried about one of these old tunnels collapsing on top of us. It doesn't look like anyone's been in here for at least a hundred years and those timbers look half rotten."

"Don't worry about them," said Joe breezily. "They built these tunnels to last. Look at this, solid as a rock." He gave one of the supporting beams a hefty kick to prove his point.

"I'm not sure that's such a good idea," began Max. Then he stopped.

There was a loud groan from the old timbers and a shower of dust fell from the tunnel roof. "Joe, what have you done?" said Lucy. "I told you it wasn't safe. We should—"

Her next words were lost in the sounds of splintering and cracking as one of the supporting timbers broke in the center. The large beam crashed to the tunnel floor and there was a deafening roar as rock and earth cascaded from the roof. Max froze in horror as a second beam toppled toward him,

an instant before Lucy crashed into him and knocked him out of the way.

The roar of falling rock subsided and gave way to dust and coughing and darkness.

Joe fumbled for his flashlight and snapped on the beam. At first he could see nothing but dust, but then the beam picked out a familiar figure, her face streaked with grime. "Charlie," he croaked. "Are you all right?"

Charlie was huddled against the far wall of the tunnel, hugging Sherlock closely to her chest. She coughed. "I swallowed a load of dust," she said in a hoarse voice. "But we're both okay. What happened? Where are the others?"

Joe swung the flashlight beam around the tunnel and illuminated a wall of rock and earth and broken timbers. He looked up at the collapsed roof and felt cold as though someone had poured ice water down his spine. "Oh, no," he gasped, "Max and Lucy are behind there. You don't think they're..." His voice tailed off.

The next sentence was too awful to say out loud.

Charlie jumped up from the floor and began to pull at the rocks and timbers that had fallen into the tunnel. "Max!" she yelled. "Lucy! Can you hear us?"

Joe joined in, clawing at the earth with his bare hands and even Sherlock began barking and digging at rubble with his front paws. "It's hopeless," sobbed Joe. "The tunnel's come down on top of them and it's all my fault."

"Shut up!" snapped Charlie. "I think I heard something." She stopped digging and pressed her ear against the wall of earth. "There," she said. "Someone's tapping."

Joe wiped his nose and listened. Almost immediately he heard a faint tapping on the rock. "I heard it too!" he cried. "Max! Lucy! Is that you?"

"Joe, I'm here," came a faint voice. It sounded muffled but it was definitely Max. "Look up near the roof of the tunnel."

Joe shone the flashlight at the roof and saw

a space where the debris hadn't quite blocked the tunnel. He scrambled up the slope of loose rock and found a small gap near the roof. On the other side he could see Max's grimy face peering back at him.

"Max!" he cried. "Are you all right? Where's Lucy?"

"I'm here too," said Lucy's voice. Her face appeared next to Max. They both looked wide-eyed and scared.

"We're okay," said Max. "Just a bit shaken up, that's all. What about you guys?"

"We're all fine," said Charlie, peering through the narrow space. "But the tunnel's blocked and we can't get to you."

"Same here," said Lucy. "Some of the really big timber supports have fallen over and there's no way we can shift them. You'll have to go back to the castle and get help."

"Okay, okay, we will," said Joe. "I'm so glad you're all right. You just hold on and we'll go and get help. Don't go away. I mean, I know you can't go away but what I mean is—"

"Stop babbling, Joe," said Max. "Just get going and make sure you don't run into those men again. Somehow I don't think they'll be very interested in helping us."

"We will!" shouted Charlie. "You guys hang on there. We'll be right back."

Charlie scrambled down from the rubble and retrieved her flashlight. She called Sherlock and the two of them started back along the tunnel. "Come on, Joe," she said. "Let's get a move on."

14

THE RETURN OF THE BLACK DOG

Max waited until the voices of his friends had faded, then collapsed onto a rock with a sigh. He looked down and realized that his tie was covered in mud. "Well, that's just great," he fumed. "This is my best tie, too. Why do these things always have to happen to me?"

Lucy sat with her back to the tunnel wall and frowned at Max. "Terrible news about the tie," she said. "I'm fine by the way, thanks for asking."

Max looked at her sheepishly. "Sorry, Luce," he said. "I was just feeling sorry for myself. How's the ankle?"

Lucy felt around her ankle gently and winced when she reached a sore spot. "It's pretty painful," she said. "I landed on it badly when the roof came down."

"Sorry about that," said Max. He looked at the heavy timbers blocking the tunnel and shivered. "But thanks for pushing me out of the way when you did. If all that stuff had fallen on me it would have ruined my chances of becoming a ballet dancer for good."

Lucy smiled. "Think nothing of it," she said. "I only saved your life because I'm so terrified of your mom."

Max shook his head. "Nah, she'd have been okay about me getting squashed just as long as I'd done my math homework first."

They both laughed and the sound echoed along the tunnel.

"So, what do we do now?" asked Lucy.

"Just sit tight until the others get back, I suppose," said Max.

"I hope they don't run into those guys again," said Lucy. "Something tells me those two are really bad news."

Lucy leaned back against the tunnel wall and tried not to think too hard about the throbbing in her ankle. Although she had not admitted it to the others, she wasn't good in confined spaces. The thought of being stuck in this tunnel for any length of time gave her an anxious, spidery feeling in her chest.

She closed her eyes and tried the deep breathing exercises that her dad had taught her to relax. She took a breath, held it, and then let it out slowly. After doing this a few times, she could feel the panic begin to subside. That was better, she told herself. All she had to do now was to keep breathing and enjoy the cool air blowing against her face.

She opened her eyes. "Max?" she said.

"What is it?" asked Max.

"Did you say this tunnel was a dead end?"

"I think so," said Max.

"In that case, where's that breeze coming from?"

Charlie, Sherlock and Joe made their way cautiously back along the tunnel. Joe kept his flashlight under his T-shirt so that it only cast a dim light, just bright enough to see by.

"Wait a minute," Charlie said, placing a hand on Joe's arm. Around a bend in the tunnel they could see the glow of the electric lights and hear the low murmuring of voices. They held their breath to listen and Charlie held Sherlock's collar to keep him still.

"I couldn't find 'em, Topper," said the first voice, who they guessed was the big man called Levi. "I looked everywhere. Those kids were probably just mucking about."

"Well, the boss was furious when I mentioned it," said Topper's rasping tones. "Wants to come down here and check it out. I wouldn't like to be in their shoes, let me tell you."

Joe jerked on Charlie's sleeve and pointed to a nearby tunnel that had one of Lucy's chalk arrows on the wall. Joe grinned. "That's the one," he whispered. "Come on, let's get out of here."

They tiptoed along the brick passage with Charlie leading until they were far enough away to be out of hearing of the two men. Then they broke into a shuffling run.

"Ow," gasped Joe. "I smacked my head on the ceiling again. I think it's bleeding."

"Keep the noise down," hissed Charlie. "Your head doesn't matter right now. We've got to get help for Max and Lucy. Look, I think we're here."

They had arrived at the bottom of the shaft with the iron rungs. Joe went up first, clambering hand over hand to the top. When he reached the top, he let down the basket on the rope for Sherlock. Charlie placed the little dog inside and gave him some pieces of cracker to keep him busy, then she watched as Joe hauled the basket back to the top.

A few minutes later, when Charlie clambered out of the top of the shaft, the first thing she did was pull her phone from her pocket and squint at the old-fashioned display. "It's no good," she said. "I still haven't got signal on this thing. We'll have to go inside and use the landline to call the police."

Joe did not reply.

"Joe?" Charlie looked up and saw that he was staring at something in the shadows. Sherlock was growling and the hackles on the back of his neck were raised into stiff spikes.

"What's wrong with you two—" she began. Then she stopped.

A short distance way, standing in a patch of moonlight, was the muscular shape of a huge black dog. The creature was as tall as her chest with powerful shoulders and long legs. Its yellow and red eyes glowed like embers and the light from the moon gleamed on its bone-white teeth. "Oh, no!" gasped Charlie. "It's Black Shuck!"

Lucy and Max felt their way cautiously along the old tunnel. Max wet a finger and held it out in front of him. "You were right. I can definitely feel a draft now, Luce," he said. "It must be coming from somewhere outside. All we have to do is follow it and we'll find our way out of here."

Lucy looked up at the old timbers anxiously. "Okay, but let's go slowly, Max," she said. "I don't want to bring the roof down on our heads again."

Max shone his flashlight along the passage in front of them. Something looked wrong with the tunnel but the air was too thick with dust and it was difficult to see. Then he realized what it was. "The tunnel floor has collapsed," he said. "Look, there's nothing but a big hole here."

Directly ahead of them lay a nine-foot-wide crater where the floor of the tunnel had fallen away. Showers of sand and small rocks fell continuously into the hole as they stood at the edge and peered in. "The dirt is fresh here," said Max, picking up a clod of earth. "And some of those timbers look like they've only just been split. I think this must have happened at the same time as the roof fell in."

Lucy gave a disappointed sigh. "Well, so much for our way out of here," she said. "We'll never get across that gap."

"Maybe we don't have to," said Max thoughtfully. He shone his flashlight down into the hole and swung it carefully around the sides of the crater. "That draft is coming from down there, I think. Maybe the tunnel collapse opened up another way out of here. Look at that!"

At the bottom of the hole, Max's flashlight beam picked out a crude arch of stones, partially covered by a fall of earth. He squatted down to get a closer look. "There's definitely a passageway down there and I'm betting it leads to somewhere in the castle grounds." He sat down on the edge of the hole and swung his legs over the side.

"Wait a minute," said Lucy, alarmed. "You're not planning to go down there, are you?"

Max shrugged. "Sure," he said. "Who knows how long it will take Joe and Charlie to get help. That's if they even manage to get past our two friends back there. Trust me, Luce, this is our best bet for getting out of here."

Lucy had not given much thought to how long it might take Joe and Charlie to get help, but now that she did, she saw that Max was right. It could take hours. She felt the spidery legs in her chest again and swallowed hard.

"All right then," she said. "We'll take a look. But on one condition."

"What's that?" asked Max.

"I'll go first. I really don't want to have to explain this to your mom."

The dark hound came out of the shadows and padded softly toward them, watching them intently all the while. When the brute was no more than ten paces from Joe and Charlie, it stopped and sniffed at the air.

"It's Black Shuck," quavered Joe in a desperate whisper. "What are we going to do? He's going to take our souls to hell."

"Whatever you do, don't make any sudden movements," said Charlie quietly. "You might scare him."

"*I* might scare *him?*" squeaked Joe.

The black dog growled. The growl was low and sounded like it came from the bottom of a very deep and dark place. Joe felt his insides turn to ice water and his legs began to shake. He didn't think he could run now, even if he wanted to.

But there was one of them who was not afraid. As soon as Black Shuck began to growl, Sherlock positioned himself in front of the children, baring his teeth and growling every bit as fiercely.

The black dog looked down at his tiny adversary and the yellow eyes narrowed. He sank back on powerful haunches as though he was preparing to leap. "Sherlock, be careful," hissed Charlie.

But Sherlock paid her no attention. He planted his four paws firmly in the grass as though nothing in the world would move him. Then, just when it looked like the two dogs would throw themselves at each other in a hugely mismatched fight,

a curious thing happened. Sherlock began to wag his tail.

At first, the great Black Shuck looked confused. He peered down at his small opponent, then, very cautiously he lowered his great head toward the little dog and sniffed. Sherlock reached up so that their muzzles were nearly touching and then he licked Black Shuck on the end of his nose. For a moment the big dog looked taken aback. Then he began to wag his own thick tail and he licked the top of Sherlock's head.

Joe's jaw dropped open. "Well," he gasped. "Will you look at that?"

Charlie said nothing, but she took a cautious step toward the two dogs.

"Charlie!" hissed Joe. "What are you doing?"

"I'm going to make friends," said Charlie.

"Are you nuts?" said Joe. "You don't know what that beast might do."

But Charlie wasn't listening. She approached Black Shuck, holding out the back of her hand toward the big dog. For a moment, the suspicion returned to the dog's eyes. He sniffed at Charlie's outstretched hand. Then he licked it gently.

Charlie ran her hand over Black Shuck's great head, rubbing him behind the ears, the way that Sherlock liked. The big dog whined with pleasure and his tail began to wag again. Then he sat down and gazed up at Charlie with trust in his eyes.

Charlie turned and grinned at Joe, who was still staring in amazement with his mouth wide open. "See?" said Charlie. "I always said Sherlock was a good judge of character. It looks like Black Shuck just wanted to make friends." She bent down to stroke her own faithful pet. "Who's a smart boy, then?" she said.

Joe swallowed and stepped forward to get a better look at the big dog. "He doesn't look so much like a demon-dog now," he said, taking care not to get too close. "In fact, he looks like an ordinary dog."

"He *is* an ordinary dog," said Charlie. "Even if he

is a very big one." She ran her hand over Black Shuck's thick fur while the big dog looked up at her just as adoringly as Sherlock had ever done.

"I think he's a Rottweiler," she said. "But look at this." She held up her hand, which was covered in something black. "Somebody has dyed his fur to cover up his brown parts. And I don't think his eyes are yellow at all. Somebody's put contact lenses in them."

Joe stared. "You can make a dog wear contact lenses?" he said. "Why on earth would anybody do a thing like that?"

Charlie shrugged. "To make him look less like an ordinary dog, I suppose," she said. "I think someone has deliberately disguised him to look like Black Shuck."

"But why?" asked Joe.

"I'm not sure," said Charlie. "Perhaps they were trying to scare people away. But they couldn't fool Sherlock, could they, boy?"

Joe smiled as he watched the girl making a fuss

of both dogs. "Well, I'm glad we solved the mystery of Black Shuck. But we still have to get help."

"There's no phone signal out here," said Charlie. "You go and use the phone inside the castle. I'll stay out here and make sure our 'demon-dog' doesn't get up to any more mischief."

Joe left Charlie with the two dogs and hurried back along the path to the front of the castle. He mounted the steps and let himself into the Great Hall where the phone was kept. Then he grabbed the old receiver and held it to his ear. There was no sound.

He tapped on the phone cradle several times but, to his dismay, the phone was completely dead. Then he saw the loose wire hanging from the bottom of the phone.

The phone line had been cut.

Joe did not have time to think about who might have done such a thing. He pulled out his own phone but there was still no signal. He looked around the room desperately. He needed to

206

summon help urgently, but he had no idea how. He thought about running to Miss Pollock's house but he didn't know where she lived and he couldn't afford to waste time looking.

Then he spotted the thick velvet-covered rope hanging in the corner of the room. Of course! The bell that was used to warn of approaching enemies. If he rang it then someone was bound to hear and come to help.

He crossed the room and yanked on the thick rope. It took a few moments to set the bell swinging but then a great booming clang sounded from the tower high above him in the castle. He kept pulling on the rope and the mournful bell rang out, echoing through the empty rooms and hallways.

Joe rang the bell until his arms ached. Then he stepped back, staring at the swinging rope as the sound of the old bell faded away. He wondered how far the sound would carry and whether anyone would answer its call. As silence took hold of the room, a voice behind him made him jump.

"What are you doing, exactly?"

Joe spun around to see the Reverend Harriet Graves standing behind him. The relief at seeing someone he knew washed over him. "Reverend Graves!" he cried. "Thank goodness you came, I'm so pleased to see you. I was ringing the bell because my friends are in trouble. You see, we found Cecilia Ufford's secret map of the tunnels beneath your chapel. But there's a gang trying to steal Ragnar's Gold and there was a cave-in and Max and Lucy are trapped. Now someone called 'the boss' is coming and..."

He stopped in mid-sentence. Joe realized that the vicar was no longer wearing her jolly expression and her mouth was set into a hard line. The black-framed glasses were gone and her eyes were cold.

"So, you found a secret map, did you? That's very interesting, young man." She glanced around the room and her eyes settled on the crossed swords hanging above the fireplace. Joe's eyes widened as he watched the vicar reach up and grasp one of the short swords, pulling it free of the wall. She held it in her hand for a moment, turning it this way and that as she admired the gleaming steel blade.

Joe swallowed. "I don't think you should do that," he said nervously. "It doesn't belong to you. You should—"

"Shut up!" The vicar's voice was so sudden and sharp that Joe jumped visibly. Then she gave an icy smile and advanced on Joe with the sword still in her hand. "Perhaps you'd better sit down and tell me all about it."

15

THE GOLDEN MASK

Trying not to put too much weight on her ankle, Lucy lowered herself over the side of the hole and scrambled down the loose earth to the bottom. She crouched down and shone her flashlight through the rough stone arch as Max peered down.

"What can you see?" he said impatiently.

"Not much," said Lucy. "There's a short passage and then it seems to open out. You were right, though, there's definitely a draft coming through here. I'm going in to take a look."

She began to crawl through the low passage on her hands and knees, holding the flashlight in her teeth. At the far end, she climbed out and found she was able to stand up. The space she was standing in was cool and dry and there were flat stones laid on the ground.

"Found anything?" Max's voice sounded muffled and distant.

"Not really," she called back. "I'm in some sort of chamber." She swung her flashlight around but the beam was too faint to see much. "My batteries are going," she said, banging the flashlight on the palm of her hand, "I can hardly see anything."

There was the sound of puffing and gasping as Max emerged from the passage and spilled ungracefully onto the floor of the chamber. "That's the last time I send you in first," he said. "A person could die of frustration waiting to hear from you."

He shone his own flashlight around and illuminated a round chamber. A mound of smooth stones had been piled in the center.

"Where are we?" said Lucy. "This doesn't look like any of the tunnels we were in before. Somehow this feels much older."

Max nodded. Lucy was right. The chamber had been made from smooth stones that had been carefully carved to fit closely together. The stones were cool and dry and, despite the faint breeze, the place felt like it had lain undisturbed for a very long time.

They stepped away from the entrance and began to feel their way around the walls. The stones were uniformly smooth and there was no obvious way out, other than the passage they had entered through.

"Ouch!" Lucy's cry echoed around the chamber and something crashed and jingled across the stone floor.

"Lucy, are you okay?" cried Max.

Lucy sat on the floor, her face contorted in pain, clutching her ankle. "I fell over something heavy," she said. "Oh boy, that really hurt."

Max shone the flashlight around the floor and inhaled sharply at what he saw. A small metal casket that had been sitting on the floor of the chamber now lay open on its side. Scattered across the flagstones were hundreds of tiny gold coins, catching the light of the flashlight beam.

"Lucy, look at this!" he gasped. "Coins! Just like the ones we saw earlier. But there must be hundreds of them in this box."

Lucy forgot the pain in her ankle and her jaw dropped open as she stared at the tiny gold discs. Each one was stamped with a cross on one side and a man's head on the other, just like the one they had found in Cecilia Ufford's box.

"It's a treasure chest!" she said in a whisper. "There must be a fortune here. Do you think there are any more boxes like this?"

Max swung the flashlight around. On top of the stones in the center of the chamber, something caught his eye that made him let out a shriek and drop the flashlight.

"What is it?" said Lucy. "What's the matter with you?"

Max pointed. "U-up th-there," he stammered.

"There's something looking down at us."

Lucy picked up his flashlight and turned toward the stones. Leaning at the base of the pile was a round shield, inlaid with gold. Standing next to it was what looked like a short sword, its blade rough and corroded but with golden decorations on the hilt. But sitting above that was something truly extraordinary.

On top of the stone pile was a large domed helmet with a face plate made of iron and gold. The black spaces for the eyeholes really did make it look like an ancient warrior was staring down at them.

"Max!" she gasped. "Look at this stuff. The coins, the sword, the shield, and the helmet. Do you realize what this all means?" She turned to Max, her eyes wide. "It's the treasure everyone has been looking for all these years. We've found Ragnar's Gold!"

The Reverend Harriet Graves grabbed Joe by the collar with her free hand and her face twisted into an ugly snarl. "Where are your friends?" she demanded. She shook him with such surprising strength that his teeth rattled.

"I-I told you," Joe stammered. "M-my f-friends are stuck in the tunnel. They n-need h-help."

"Is there anyone else here?"

Joe glanced at the gleaming sword in the vicar's hand. His mouth had become as dry as old leather and his voice sounded shaky when he spoke. "N-no," he gasped. "N-no one."

"I knew it," growled the vicar. "When my boys said they saw four children and a dog in the tunnels, I knew it had to be the same kids who told me they were staying at the castle."

"Your boys?" Realization was beginning to dawn on Joe. "Then you must be the one those two men were waiting for. The one they called the boss!"

She gave a cruel smile. "That's what they call me," she said. "Topper and Levi aren't the brightest pair but at least they do what their mother tells them."

"Their mother?" Joe could scarcely believe what he was hearing. "You mean Topper and Levi are your sons?"

The vicar laughed at the confused expression on Joe's face. "Very good," she said. "I can tell you're not the brains in your gang. Now tell me about this map you found. Where is it?"

Joe swallowed hard. "Downstairs, in the kitchen," he blurted. "Max made a copy of it before we went out."

"Show me!" the vicar dragged Joe across the room and shoved him, stumbling, down the winding stairs to the kitchen. When Joe showed her the metal box and the map that Max had copied out, the vicar's eyes gleamed greedily.

She shoved Joe into a chair, then stuck the sword into the wide belt of her trousers while she snatched up the paper. "Of course, of course," she muttered to herself as she traced a finger across the lines. "The letter V must mark the place. Moldering corpses, we've been digging in the wrong place all this time!"

"So, it's true, then?" said Joe. "You're looking for Ragnar's Gold, and then you're going to sell it, aren't you?" Now she was no longer holding the sword, Joe was starting to feel a bit braver.

The vicar narrowed her eyes. "You really have been poking around in my business, haven't you?" she said. Joe wondered how he had ever thought that the Reverend Graves looked jolly.

"Well, you're right," she continued. "I've been looking for Ragnar's Gold ever since I first found those tunnels ten years ago. I knew the treasure was down there somewhere, but I just didn't know where. But now I've got this"—she held up Max's map—"I'll find that treasure and have it out of the country within the next two days."

She reached into her jacket pocket and pulled out something that Joe recognized as a short-wave radio, similar to the one his dad used on their motorboat. When she pressed a button, the radio crackled to life.

"Topper!" she barked. "Where are you?"

There was a hiss of static and Topper's weasely voice came over the radio. "Is that you, Ma?"

he said. "Me and Levi are still in the chapel, but there's no sign of the kids."

"You're a pair of idiots!" she snapped. "I've got their ringleader right here. And I've got something else, too—a map! It's going to take us straight to the gold. Meet me in the tunnels in twenty minutes and we'll have that treasure out of the ground in no time." She clicked off the radio and returned the device to her pocket with a smile.

"You can't just take it," said Joe. "Treasure like that should be in a museum. Besides, I thought vicars weren't supposed to steal."

The Reverend Graves looked puzzled for a moment. Then she glanced down and started laughing. "Oh, you mean this?" she said, pulling off the dog collar. "This disguise is very useful for getting rid of unwanted visitors. After all, no one ever suspects a vicar, do they? Hattie Graves is my name, though most people just call me Ma."

Joe gulped and wondered what it would be like to grow up with Hattie Graves as your mother.

"And what about Black Shuck?" he said. "I suppose he belongs to you as well, does he?"

Ma Graves cackled. "He belongs to me, all right," she said. "It was a stroke of genius, getting a big dog and disguising him as Black Shuck. All I had to do was spin some tall story about how he lurks in the forest and everyone is terrified to come near the place after dark. It means we can work in peace."

Ma Graves seemed very pleased with herself and looked like she would have gone on boasting about her cleverness but at that moment there was the sound of a tinkling bell from the floor above. She gave a start and looked up at the stairs. "What was that?" she said. "Who's up there?"

"It's the front door," said Joe. "I think there's somebody outside."

Ma Graves pulled the sword from her belt, looking wild-eyed and twitchy like a startled animal.

"Are you expecting anyone?" she hissed.

Joe shook his head.

Whoever was at the door was not about to go away. The bell rang again and again. Then someone began hammering on the wood. Ma Graves pulled Joe out of the chair by his collar. "All right, you," she growled. "Answer the door and get rid of them. And don't try anything clever. I'll be standing right behind you with this." She brandished the sword for effect.

Joe allowed himself to be led upstairs. Ma Graves positioned herself behind the oak door so she couldn't be seen and then nodded at Joe to open it.

Joe opened the door a crack and peered out. Standing on the doorstep and looking very stern was the tall, upright figure of Mary Pollock. "About time, too," said Miss Pollock, when she saw him. "I've been ringing that bell for the last five minutes. What on earth is the matter with you, boy? You look like you've seen a ghost!"

Joe gulped. From the corner of his eye he could

see Ma Graves standing behind the door with the sword in her hand. "Oh, er, h-hello, Miss Pollock," he said, turning on a tight smile. "I'm fine thank you. I've just been asleep, that's all."

"I see." Miss Pollock raised an eyebrow. "And what about your friends? Are they here too?" She tried to peer around the door, but Joe stood firmly in the way.

"Oh, no, they're out at the moment. I'm the only one here. Just me. Nobody else at all." Joe bit his lip to stop himself from babbling.

"Really?" Miss Pollock's eyebrow rose a little higher. "Then who was ringing the bell earlier?"

Joe stared. He had forgotten all about having rung the bell in the tower. "Oh," he said. "That. Well, yes. That was me."

Miss Pollock frowned. "I thought you were asleep?"

"Yes, I am. I mean, I was. I mean, I must have done it in my sleep. I have a terrible habit of sleepwalking." Joe was beginning to feel hot and bothered. "I do all sorts of things when I'm asleep. Once I got up in the night and washed all the windows in the house. I couldn't remember a thing about it in the morning." He grinned in what he hoped was a convincing way.

Miss Pollock leveled her steely gaze on him and Joe fell silent. "Well," she said eventually. "I came over because I was concerned there might be something wrong. But if you're sure everything is alright?"

"Oh, yes, Miss Pollock," stammered Joe. "Everything's just fine, thank you for asking. Sorry for the inconvenience."

"I'll be off then," said Miss Pollock, turning to go. Then she stopped and turned back. "Oh, I meant to ask you," she said. "How was your visit to the chapel this afternoon? Did you find what you were looking for?"

Joe blinked. "Oh, that," he said. "Yes, thank you, Miss Pollock. The vicar was very helpful."

Miss Pollock stared. "Really?" she said. "I'm very glad to hear it. Well, good night, then."

"Good night, Miss Pollock."

"Hot milk and nutmeg," said Miss Pollock as she turned to go.

"I'm sorry?"

"Drink a glass before you go to bed," she said. "It's the perfect cure for sleepwalking. Never fails."

"Th-thank you. I will."

Miss Pollock went down the steps without looking back and Joe closed the door gratefully. "She's gone," he said with a relieved sigh.

"Lucky for you," croaked Ma Graves, sticking the sword back in her belt. "Now, is there another way out of here?"

"There's a back staircase in the kitchen," said Joe. "Why? What are you going to do with me?"

Ma Graves gave Joe a thin smile. "I haven't come this far to have you ruin my plans," she said. "I'm taking you back to the chapel and then we're going to take care of you and your little friends. Oh, don't look so worried," she said. "I'm not a murderer. I'm just going to keep you all tied up in the tunnels for a couple of days until I've got the treasure out of the country. As long as you all behave yourselves, you've got nothing to worry about. Now, get moving!"

She dragged Joe back down to the kitchen and then shoved him up the stairs to the rear door. She pulled the sword from her belt and opened the door cautiously. "It looks like that old witch has gone," she said. "But go quietly. I don't want to attract any more attention."

It was dark outside and neither of them had a flashlight, but the moon was full and they could see quite clearly in the silvery light. Ma Graves led them around the castle in the direction of the forest. As they approached the trees, she stopped and peered into the darkness.

"What's that?" she hissed. "Something moved, over there by those trees."

Joe looked at the deep shadows where the woman was pointing and noticed a patch of darkness that seemed deeper than the surrounding shadow. As he watched, he could make out the powerful body and broad haunches of a large, black dog.

Ma Graves smiled. "It's just Shuck," she said. "I let him loose earlier. Get over here, you."

Black Shuck did not move. The yellow eyes glowered at the woman and the great dog bared its teeth and snarled.

"I said get over here, you beastly animal!" snapped Ma.

The dog growled and started to come toward them. Ma Graves looked suddenly alarmed. "Stay back," she ordered. "Stay back, or you'll regret it." She took another step backward. "All right, you brute, don't say I didn't warn you."

She fumbled with the sword, but the handle had become stuck in her belt and she tugged on it frantically, trying to pull it free. As Ma struggled with the ancient weapon, there was a scampering of small paws across the grass as something small and white streaked toward Ma.

Before Ma could pull out the sword, Sherlock leaped at the woman and fastened his sharp little teeth onto the sleeve of her jacket. Ma let out a shriek and began to shake her arm in a frantic attempt to get him off but Sherlock would not let go, snarling and growling as he dangled from her jacket cuff.

Then came the sound of ripping material and Sherlock fell to the ground, the end of Ma Graves's sleeve still clutched in his teeth. Now Ma was pulling at the sword again. "You little rat," she screeched. "I'll teach you a lesson."

She yanked the sword free of her belt but, scarcely a heartbeat later, Shuck's great bulk crashed into her. Ma Graves was knocked to the ground and the sword went spinning from her hand. Ma writhed helplessly on the muddy grass, pinned under the weight of the big dog. "Get him off me!" she shrieked. "Please, somebody. He's going to eat me alive!"

Joe stared at the terrified woman, fighting with

her own dog, and wondered if he should try to help.

"Hey, Joe!" shouted a voice from the trees.

Joe looked up to see Charlie running toward him. "Come on!" she yelled. "Before she gets up again. Start running!"

16

TREASURE HUNTERS

Charlie ran past Joe, with Sherlock at her heels. "Get moving!" she cried.

Joe took a last look at Ma Graves, still struggling under the weight of Black Shuck, then turned and ran after Charlie. "Where are we going?" he panted.

"As far away as possible from that woman!" yelled Charlie. "Hurry up, while Shuck's still keeping her occupied."

Joe looked back again but there was no one chasing them. He slowed to a walk. "That was a great idea to set Black Shuck on her," he said. "How did you manage to get him to do that?"

"I didn't," said Charlie. "Shuck decided to do it

all by himself." She frowned. "I'm pretty sure someone had been mistreating him. I found marks on his back where he'd been beaten with a stick. As soon as he saw the Reverend Graves, he just went for her."

"And Sherlock joined in too," said Joe. "Good old Sherlock." He bent down to rub behind the little dog's ears. "I swear he's as brave as a lion."

"No way," said Charlie. "He's braver than ten lions."

The sound of loud barking made them stop and turn around. Then came a shriek, followed by the sounds of whimpering. "Oh no," gasped Charlie. "Shuck! That dreadful woman has hurt him, I know she has. We have to go back."

Joe bit his lip. "We can't go back, Charlie. Ma still has the sword. And besides, we have to get help for Max and Lucy."

Poor Charlie looked deeply unhappy at the thought that Shuck might have been hurt and it was all Joe could do to persuade her to start moving again. "Come on," he said gently.

"We really have to get going now."

Charlie looked around and turned pale. "Where's Sherlock gone?" she said. "He was here just a moment ago. You don't think he's gone back to look for Shuck, do you?"

By way of a reply there was a familiar bark from the other direction. "That was Sherlock," said Joe. "He must have gone on ahead. Let's get after him."

They started off again, following the sound of Sherlock's barking. "This is ridiculous," said Joe. "I can hear him, but I can't see him anywhere. Where could he have gone?"

The moon came out from behind a cloud, casting a silver light over the field. Directly in front of them was a rounded shape that looked like a beached whale in the middle of the field.

"It's the old burial chamber," said Joe.

There was another bark, muffled this time, and slightly echoey. It seemed to be coming from inside the mound. "He's gotten inside the chamber," said Charlie. "What's he up to?"

At the far end of the burial mound, they found the low arch where they had sat while Miss Pollock had told them the story of Ragnar's Gold. The sound of Sherlock's barking was echoing loudly from inside.

"It's all right, Sherlock!" shouted Charlie. "I'm coming." She ducked low and squeezed through the narrow entrance, quickly disappearing from view.

Joe waited outside, watching for any sign of Ma Graves. When Charlie didn't emerge, he shouted through the entrance, "You okay in there?"

"I don't know what's gotten into him," called back Charlie. "He keeps running around in circles like he's gone nuts. I could use a bit of help in here."

Joe sighed. He wasn't sure if he was more worried about going inside a thousand-year-old burial mound at night or staying outside and getting caught by Ma Graves. Reluctantly he crouched down and followed Charlie inside.

The air inside the burial chamber smelled earthy and deeply chilled like a place that has not seen the sun for a very long time. Charlie was standing in the middle of the chamber, trying to grab Sherlock as he scampered around her in tight circles. Every so often Sherlock would run to a corner of the chamber and scrabble frantically at the floor.

Charlie gave Joe an exasperated look. "He keeps scratching in that corner," she said. "Maybe he smells a rabbit or something. Help me get him outside."

Joe approached Sherlock and saw that the little dog was scratching at the earth and had uncovered a flat slab of stone. "I don't think it's a rabbit," said Joe. "Shine your flashlight over here for a minute."

He kneeled down and brushed away the rest of the earth around the slab. He was surprised to see that there was a clear gap around the stone and that there was a soft breath of air coming through the gap.

"Look at this," he said. "There's something down there."

Charlie crouched down as Sherlock continued

to snuffle around the edges of the stone. "What sort of something?" she asked.

"I'm not sure," said Joe. "But there's air coming through this gap. I think there might be a space underneath here."

Charlie frowned. "That's impossible. Miss Pollock said this burial mound had been here for centuries. If there was something underneath it, people would have found it before now."

"Not necessarily," said Joe. "Perhaps no one ever looked closely before. Do you remember Max's map? He said the tunnels came all the way out to the burial mound. What if there's another way into the tunnels from here? We might be able to get to Max and Lucy this way."

Charlie looked dubious. "That's a real long shot, Joe," she said. "We have no idea where Max and Lucy are."

"Help me to lift this stone so we can find out," pleaded Joe. "Come on, what have we got to lose?"

Charlie kneeled down, next to Joe. "All right, what do you want me to do?"

"Just hook your fingers under the stone here," he said. "Then both together, one, two, three... *heave!*"

They pulled against the stone with all their strength. Joe gritted his teeth and Charlie planted her foot against the wall to brace herself. They pulled until their fingers felt like they might break but the stone still refused to budge.

"It's no good," gasped Charlie, sitting back on the floor. "It's too heavy and we're wasting time. Let's go and find Miss Pollock's house and ask if we can use her phone." She got up to leave and then stopped and stared at Joe. "Did you hear that?"

It had been the tiniest of noises, like the sound a mouse might make scratching on a kitchen floor. But it had come from somewhere underneath the stone.

"What was that?" said Joe. "Is there somebody under there?"

The next noise was sudden and hard: the unmistakable sound of a rock being struck against the underside of the stone. Charlie and Joe stared at it in amazement. It sounded like someone was trying to get out.

Joe put his mouth close to the stone. "H-hello?" he said. "Is there anyone down there?"

"Joe?" The voice was muffled and indistinct through the thick stone. "Joe, are you up there?"

Joe's eyes widened. "Max?" he said. "Max, is that you?"

There was an excited yell from under the stone. "Joe! Yes, it's me, Max. I'm in here with Lucy. We're okay, but we can't get out."

"The stone's too heavy for us," came Lucy's voice. "Can you lift it?"

"We already tried," called Joe. "I think we might need to get someone else to help us."

At that moment, Sherlock began to bark. Joe and Charlie both turned to see a bulky figure squeezing through the narrow entrance and blocking the light from outside. When the person stood up in the chamber, Joe groaned. It was Ma Graves.

Her jacket was torn and she was covered in mud and her hair stood out like a brush, but she was still holding the sword. She looked at Joe and Charlie and curled her lip. "Thought you'd escaped, did you?" she said.

Sherlock positioned himself in front of the children and bared his teeth at the woman. Ma looked startled and took a step backward, holding the sword out in front of her. "Keep that animal under control," she snarled.

Charlie darted forward and grabbed Sherlock's collar, then retreated, keeping her eyes on the sword all the time. "I'm not surprised Sherlock doesn't like you," she said. "I saw what you did to poor Shuck. Somebody ought to beat *you* with a stick and see how much you like it."

Ma Graves laughed. "Shuck was useful, but he was becoming a handful," she said. "Better keep your dog under control or I'll do the same to him."

Charlie pulled Sherlock closer. "You're a monster!" she cried. "Shuck was faithful to you and all you did was treat him horribly. People like you belong in jail."

Ma Graves scowled and jerked her head toward the entrance. "Get outside, both of you," she said. "And don't try any funny business because my boys are out there."

She paused and cocked her head to one side. The unmistakeable sounds of hammering were coming from a stone slab in the corner. Joe groaned inwardly. *Please, Max,* he thought, *don't make a noise. Not now.*

There was a muffled shout from under the stone. "Hey, Joe," came Max's voice. "Are you getting us out of here or what?"

Ma's eyes widened and she took three quick paces across the chamber to the flagstone. "Who is that?" she said. "Is there someone down there?"

Joe tried to smile innocently but only succeeded in looking like he was in pain. "I didn't hear anything," he said. "Perhaps it was just an echo?"

"That's no echo," snapped Ma. "Tell me who's down there or I'll make you both sorry."

"Hey, Joe!" shouted Max's voice again. "You'll never believe what we've found down here. There's a whole box of golden coins and a golden helmet too."

Joe and Charlie exchanged a pained glance as Ma Graves's eyes grew round. "Gold?" she repeated. Then a slow smile spread across her face and she gave a nasty chuckle. "Well, I guess this is my lucky day after all."

She bent down at the entrance and yelled outside. "Topper, Levi! Get yourselves in here, boys, and bring the tools. We've found Ragnar's Gold!"

17

DEN OF THIEVES

Two more figures squeezed through the narrow entrance. First came Topper, carrying a pickaxe and a big flashlight that flooded the chamber with a fierce white light. He was followed by Levi, struggling to fit his bulk through the entrance as he hauled another pickaxe, a crowbar, and several large sacks.

Topper gazed around the chamber and gave a whistle. "Wow, look at this place. I thought that old chapel was creepy, but this gives me the chills."

The peace of the chamber was shattered by Levi dumping his tools on the stone floor with a crash.

"Careful, you great ox," snapped Ma. "This place is over a thousand years old. Show a bit of respect."

"Thousand years old, my backside," growled Levi. "That stuff weighs a ton. What are we doing in here anyway, Ma?"

Ma Graves smiled indulgently at her sons. "Take a look under that stone in the corner, boys," she said. "There's gold down there."

The two men stared at Ma as though she had told them the moon was made of cheese. Levi looked suspiciously at Charlie and Max. "Are you sure about this, Ma? Those are two of the kids we caught earlier. Are you sure they aren't just pulling your leg?"

The smile disappeared from Ma Graves's face and her eyes became as hard as flint. "I've spent ten years researching this place," she snarled at Levi. "Are you trying to tell me you know more about Ragnar's Gold than your ma?"

Levi held up his hands defensively. "N-no, Ma," he stammered.

"Good," said Ma. "Now get that stone lifted."

Levi scuttled away and grabbed a crowbar from the floor. Wedging the bar between the gaps in the flagstone, he put his full weight behind it. For a moment, nothing happened, then, all at once, the big stone came free with a wet, sucking noise.

They craned to get a better look as Levi and Topper hauled up the stone. Sure enough, underneath it was a round hole, the width of a man.

"You were right, Ma," said Topper. "There is something down there."

Ma Graves and her two boys drew closer and peered into the hole, then jumped back. Topper shrieked and made a short dash toward the exit and Levi held the crowbar out in front of him. "Argh!" he cried. "There's a ghost in a shirt and tie down there."

Ma Graves was clearly made of sterner stuff than her sons. She looked down into the hole and then frowned. "You idiots," she said. "It's just more kids."

"It's Max and Lucy," said Charlie quickly. "They

242

were trapped in the tunnels. They're not going to hurt you."

Levi lowered his crowbar and looked into the hole again. He blinked with surprise as two very dirty faces peered back at him. "Er, hello there," said Max, looking up at Topper's surprised face. "Sorry to bother you. But I think we took a wrong turn down there somewhere."

"Get them out of there," said Ma. "Quickly."

"Grab hold," grunted Levi. He reached into the hole and took Max's outstretched hand, then pulled him straight out of the hole in one movement.

Max blinked in the light of the flashlight and looked around before his eyes came to rest on his friends. Then he broke into a huge grin. "Joe! Charlie!" he cried. He rushed across the chamber and threw his arms around both of them. "Thank goodness!" he gasped. "I thought we'd be stuck down there forever. You'll never believe it, but we've found Ragnar's Gold!"

Then he looked around and took in the three adults who were staring sullenly at him. "What's the Reverend Graves doing here?" he whispered.

"It's a long story," said Joe. "We'll explain later."

Levi reached down and lifted Lucy, coughing and spluttering, out of the hole. "It's so dusty down there," she gasped. "I never thought I'd see the light again. Thank goodness you...Oh!" She lapsed into silence when she saw Ma Graves and the two boys, then she looked at her friends. "I'm guessing we're not quite out of trouble yet?"

"Not quite," said Charlie. "You've got a lot to catch up on."

"Shut up, all of you," snapped Ma. "Topper, get in that hole and see what's down there."

Topper's eyes widened in fright. "What, down *there*? What about my asthma? You should send Levi."

"I'd never fit down there," said Levi. "Look at the size of me, compared to that hole."

Topper looked like a cornered animal searching

for a means of escape. "Oh, all right," he grumbled. "Help me get down."

Levi helped him into the narrow space and then handed him the flashlight. For a while they could hear Topper muttering and cursing inside the hole, then everything went quiet.

Ma and Levi gazed expectantly into the hole. In their excitement, they seemed to have forgotten all about the children. Lucy nudged Joe in the ribs. "Get ready to make a run for it," she whispered, "while they're distracted."

Very slowly the four of them began to shuffle toward the narrow entrance, moving as quietly as they could manage. "What are you lot up to?" snarled Ma. "Everybody stay where I can see 'em."

At that moment one of Topper's hands appeared over the edge of the hole, followed by his beaming face. "Ma!" he shrieked. "What the kids said, it's true! Look at this!"

He brought his fist out of the hole and flung a handful of coins high into the air, like someone throwing confetti at a wedding. The golden discs showered down on the chamber floor, clattering and tinkling as they rolled to a stop.

Ma bent down to pick up one of the coins and her eyes glittered as she stared at it. "Hell's bells," she muttered. "This coin is nearly perfect." She looked around at the golden discs scattered across the floor. "There's hundreds of them here."

"There's a whole chest full of 'em down there," said Topper with a grin. "Not to mention a golden helmet and a sword too. It's Ragnar's Gold all right, and there's more of it than we ever imagined!"

Then Ma Graves and her boys were grinning and laughing and holding up the coins to look at them in the light. "All right, enough," said Ma. "We don't have time to waste. Who knows who else those kids might have told about this." She picked up a handful of the hessian sacks and handed them to Topper.

"Take these and start filling them up with all the gold you can carry," she said. She watched Topper disappear from view and then turned to Levi. "Go and get the van, and we'll load it up and get out of here. With a bit of luck, we can still catch the midnight ferry and have all this stuff out of the country by morning."

Levi frowned at the children. "What about the kids, Ma?" he said. "They'll raise the alarm as soon as we're gone."

Ma looked at the children and a cruel smile spread across her face. "Don't worry, I've got plans for them," she said. "As soon as we've got the treasure out, we'll shove the kids back down there without a flashlight and put the stone back. They'll never get out without help." She saw the looks of horror on the faces of the children and laughed. "If you're really lucky I might even remember to phone the police at some point and tell them where you are."

Levi chuckled. "Got to hand it to you, Ma," he said. "You think of everything." He turned and began to squeeze his way out of the narrow entrance.

Lucy stared into the black hole and swallowed hard. She had managed to stay calm while she and Max had been stuck in the tunnels, but the thought of being shut in there again, for days on end, with no food or water or even a light to see by, was too horrible for words. And what if Ma never did tell the police where they were? They might be stuck in there forever. She clenched her fists tightly.

"You can't put us back in that hole," she said. "I won't go."

"You don't have a lot of choice," said Ma. "I can't take the risk that you'll give us away before we're out of the country. Don't worry, you won't be down there for more than two or three days."

Lucy's face turned red with fury. "I can't go in there," she said. "I don't like confined spaces. I won't do it."

Ma scowled, impatient now. "You're giving me a headache," she said, brandishing the sword. "Now, stop complaining or your little dog will get the same as Shuck."

Lucy bared her teeth. "Leave us alone!" she roared. She launched herself, fists flailing, at Ma. The woman tried to catch Lucy by the wrists, but the girl was too quick and kicked Ma hard in the shins.

At the same instant, Charlie released her grip on Sherlock's collar and the little dog leaped at Ma, knocking her backward so that she tripped over Max's foot, which he had stuck out behind her.

Ma flailed her arms, trying to regain her balance, but only succeeded in putting one foot down the open hole. She crashed noisily to the floor and her flashlight clattered across the stones and went out. "Now!" yelled Lucy. "Everybody run for it!"

Joe was closest to the exit. He turned and scrambled out through the archway, scraping his arms on the rough wall in his hurry to get away. Outside, the fresh air hit him and he paused, wondering which way to run. There was no use going back to the castle; the phone lines had been cut and Ma and her boys would find him

there for sure. There was only one thing for it—
he would have to try to find Miss Pollock's
house.

With a last glance back at the burial chamber,
he started to run across the field. But he had gone
no more than three steps when the darkness
exploded into daylight. A dozen flashlight beams
came on suddenly, stopping Joe in his tracks. As
he raised a hand to his eyes, more lights came on:
car headlights, together with the spooling blue
lights of a police car. Dark shadows moved around
behind the lights now, and someone was shouting
orders. "This is the police! Put up your hands and
walk forward, slowly."

Joe's brain reeled. He couldn't understand what
the police were doing here. He hadn't called them.
Had they come to arrest him?

Stunned by the lights, he took a step backward
just as Ma emerged from the chamber behind him.
The big woman was quick to react. She grabbed
Joe by the collar and pulled out her sword. "Stay

back, all of you," she yelled. "I've got the boy. If anyone tries to stop me, he'll get it."

Ma locked a muscular arm around Joe's neck and began to drag him toward the darkness of the forest. The flashlight beams followed them. "Hold your fire," shouted a voice from somewhere behind the light. "She's got a hostage."

"Keep up, boy," growled Ma, as she pulled him across the field by the scruff of his jacket. "Or I'll make you regret it."

When they reached the edge of the forest, Ma looked back to check that no one was following. "You've cost me a fortune, boy," she snarled. "But with you as a hostage, I can still get away on the midnight ferry." She shook Joe vigorously. "Just don't try anything clever, if you know what's good for you." Ma's eyes were wild with the look of a hunted creature and all traces of the kindly vicar they had first met had now disappeared.

Joe opened his mouth to say something but there was a sudden movement from the trees behind them. They turned to see a pair of fierce yellow eyes staring at them from the shadows.

"It's Shuck," gasped Joe. "He's still alive!"

The expression on Ma's face turned to pure terror. As the great dog leaped, she tried to raise her sword but Shuck knocked her down and pinned her to the ground with his front paws. The sword went spinning away into the bushes.

Joe scrambled away and began to run. Almost immediately, he ran headlong into a burly figure coming the other way holding a flashlight. He was about to scream when a reassuring voice spoke to him.

"Steady on, son," said the man. "You're safe now." Joe looked up and registered the dark blue uniform and peaked cap of a policeman.

"Oh!" said Joe in a small voice. "Thank you!"

Then the forest was filled with more light beams and more shouting. Two police officers struggled to pull Shuck off Ma while a policewoman handcuffed her hands tightly behind her back.

Several people started talking to Joe at once and someone put a blanket around his shoulders. He watched the people moving around him as though he was in a dream.

"Well done, son," the policeman said, patting him on the back. "Your friends are all safe and we've got the whole gang." Then he frowned. "You look a bit pale," he said. "Maybe you should sit down for a bit."

Joe was shivering and his legs felt wobbly, but he didn't want the policeman to know that. "Oh, don't worry about me, I'm absolutely fine, thanks," he said, forcing a smile. "It takes more than a demon-dog and a vicar with a sword to scare me."

It was only when he tried to take a step forward that he realized his legs would no longer obey the instructions he gave them. "Oh!" he said, putting out a hand to steady himself. "Maybe I will sit down. Just for a moment."

18

AN INSPECTOR CALLS

It was several minutes before Joe felt steady enough on his feet to walk back with the police officer. By the time they reached the burial mound, more police cars had arrived and their blue lights were whirling around the darkened field. Men and women, in high-visibility vests, chattered into radios and Joe spotted Levi and Topper, sitting glumly in the back of a police van, both wearing handcuffs.

Two more policemen arrived holding Ma Graves. She looked wild with rage as she was bundled into the back of a police car. Joe stared at the woman who had so recently taken him hostage, but Ma just looked straight ahead without acknowledging him at all.

Then Joe saw his friends sitting on the tailgate of a police van, wearing silver blankets around their shoulders. It was Sherlock that spotted Joe first. The little dog barked excitedly and sprinted across the grass, leaping up at Joe to be petted.

Joe laughed out loud and kneeled down to receive a thorough tongue-washing. Charlie followed close behind Sherlock. She ran up to Joe and threw her arms around him. "Joe! Thank goodness you're okay! I was so worried about you."

She squeezed him so tightly that he gasped for breath. Then, just as suddenly, she seemed to remember herself. She let go and stepped back, digging her hands deep into her jeans pockets. "Er, what I mean is," she said, "it's lucky you didn't get yourself kidnapped or anything. You've caused us enough trouble for one vacation."

Joe grinned. "Thanks, Charlie. I was worried about you too."

Max arrived, helping Lucy, who was now limping quite badly. Lucy gave Joe a hug and Max punched him affectionately on the shoulder.

"Hey, buddy," said Max with a grin. "I'm really glad you're not dead. My mom would've killed me."

Joe looked around at his friends and was surprised to find a lump forming in his throat. He drew in a deep, shuddering breath and then, as if a great weight had been lifted from his chest, he promptly burst into tears.

"Hey," said Lucy. "It's okay. Everyone's all right, and we caught the bad guys."

"*Again*," added Max. "We really have to stop making a habit of this."

Without saying anything further, the four of them reached out and embraced each other in a big hug that only ended when a small brown and white dog wriggled between their legs and began barking because he wasn't getting enough attention.

"So, I guess it's you lot I have to thank for this mess," said a stern voice. They broke apart and turned to find a severe-looking lady standing behind them. She wore a smart gray suit, and her dark hair was tied in a tight, business-like bun. There was a hard look in her eyes that suggested she was not someone that they wanted to mess with.

"My name is Detective Inspector Lewis," she said. "We had a tip-off that there was a gang plundering treasure from this site. Do you mind telling me how you're involved in all of this?"

The four children looked at each other before Max spoke up. "Well, it all started when we found the map," he said.

"And that led us to the tunnels," added Joe.

"But there was a cave-in and Max and I got trapped," said Lucy.

"And that was when we discovered Ragnar's Gold," announced Max.

"Then Ma Graves tried to trap us all inside the chamber while she made off with it," said Charlie. "But Black Shuck stopped her."

The inspector threw up her hands. "All right, that's enough!" she said. "Isn't there a grown-up here I could talk to?"

"Perhaps I could be of some help?" The inspector turned to see the prim figure of Miss Pollock, striding out of the gloom toward them. She gave the children a nod. "They told me I could find you all here. All okay, I hope? No broken bones? Excellent."

Then she turned to Inspector Lewis. "My name is Mary Pollock. I was the one who called the police. I thought something was amiss earlier on when I heard the castle bell ringing." She nodded toward Joe. "But after I spoke to this young man, I was quite certain of it. He's not much of a liar."

"Oh, he's very good at it sometimes," piped up Max. But he fell silent when Inspector Lewis glared at him.

Miss Pollock continued. "What aroused my suspicions was that he said he'd spoken to the vicar, whereas I know for a fact that we haven't had a vicar here for nearly twenty-five years. After I left the castle, I went to the chapel to investigate for myself and discovered the tools belonging to those men and some of the coins they'd dug up. It didn't take much to work out what was really going on."

"Well, you did the right thing," said Inspector Lewis. "Thank you for your assistance."

"I believe the real thanks should go to these children," said Miss Pollock. "After all, as I understand it, they're the ones who discovered Ragnar's Gold."

"I keep hearing about this gold," said the Inspector. "But I've yet to see any of it." She waved to a large policeman standing near the entrance of the burial mound who was holding a small casket in his hands. "Sergeant!" she shouted. "Bring that thing over here."

The policeman walked across the grass toward them. "That's the box I tripped over in the chamber," said Lucy excitedly.

The sergeant nodded to the inspector. "We found this inside the burial mound, ma'am. It looks like those men were in the process of removing it when we arrived. Just take a look at this." He raised the lid to reveal a gleaming pool of golden coins, shining in the rotating lights.

The inspector let out a low whistle and picked up one of the coins. "Looks like these kids were telling the truth," she said. "This is quite a haul. It must be worth thousands."

"And that's not all, ma'am," said the sergeant. "PC Dobbs says there's a load more treasure in the lower chamber. Gold, jewelry, coins, all sorts of things."

"Don't forget the golden helmet," chimed in Lucy.

"And the sword and the shield," added Max. "We found all of it."

The inspector ran a weary hand across her brow. "It looks like this case is more complicated than I thought. All right, Sergeant, see if you can find someone from the local museum to come and take a look at the evidence. As for you lot..." She turned back to the children. "I'm going to need a statement from you before I do anything else."

"Perhaps," offered Miss Pollock, "we could do

that up at the castle. Everybody looks like they could do with a nice cup of tea."

It was several hours before the inspector was satisfied that she understood the full story. They sat around the large table in the castle kitchen and the inspector made them recount the tale from the beginning, while Joe provided sausage sandwiches for everyone, including Sherlock.

The little dog had quite enjoyed himself running around all night with the children, but he couldn't understand why they seemed to have forgotten about mealtimes. He wolfed down four sausages, including the one he managed to swipe from the inspector's plate while she wasn't looking. Then he curled up on the hearth for a well-earned sleep.

The children took turns recounting their parts of the tale, taking care to leave nothing out. Charlie explained how she had discovered the box containing Cecilia Ufford's map, and Max took great pride in demonstrating how he'd decoded its meaning, pausing to make sure that the inspector spelled "steganography" correctly in her notebook. Then Lucy and Max explained how they had found Ragnar's Gold and lastly Joe and Charlie spoke about their encounter with Black Shuck and the fake vicar.

"Her real name is Hattie Graves," said the inspector. "Known as Ma Graves to her friends. It turns out that she and her boys are wanted in six different counties for stealing archaeological treasures. Ma is the real brains of the outfit; using that 'demon-dog' to scare people away was a very clever move."

"What's going to happen to Shuck now?" asked Charlie anxiously. "That woman was so cruel to him. It's not his fault that people were scared of him."

The inspector shrugged. "We'll get a vet to look at his injuries," she said. "But I don't hold out much hope of finding him a new home. You can't trust a big dog like that if it's been mistreated."

"Stuff and nonsense," said Miss Pollock at once. "There's no such thing as a bad dog, Inspector, only bad owners. That dog will be perfectly fine as long as—"

"As long as you show him who's in charge of the pack," interrupted Charlie.

Miss Pollock nodded approvingly. "Quite so," she said. "If it's all right with you, Inspector, I'd like to adopt this 'demon-dog' of yours. I'm sure he'll prove a very loyal companion once he's properly trained. Captain and I will both be glad of the company."

Charlie beamed. "Really?" she said. "You'd do that for Shuck? That's wonderful."

The inspector raised her eyebrows. "Well, I'm sure there'll be some paperwork to complete," she said. "But if you're sure?"

"Then it's settled," said Miss Pollock in a way that made it clear the matter was absolutely settled and not open to any further discussion. "I'll start

266

work with him as soon as you can bring him to my house."

"What about the gold?" asked Lucy. "What's going to happen to that?"

"That will be for the coroner to decide," said the inspector. "But a find like that should belong to the nation. It will probably end up in a museum."

"Do you think," said Joe thoughtfully, "that they might let me take some of it home for the weekend to show my mom and dad? My dad bought me a metal detector, but I've never found anything this big before. He'd be really impressed."

"Hmm, letting Joe take some priceless relics home for the weekend," said Max. "What could possibly go wrong?"

Inspector Lewis closed her notebook with a snap. "Well, that just about covers all my questions. I wish some of my officers were as talented at detective work as you lot seem to be. Perhaps you should come and see me about a job in a few years' time?"

They beamed with pride at this praise, especially Joe, who had been imagining himself with a pencil and notebook taking statements from bank robbers.

"However," said Inspector Lewis, "there's still one thing we haven't talked about. How is it that four children and a dog are living in a castle *by themselves*? Where are your parents?"

The four children exchanged guilty glances. "Our parents sort of said it would be okay," said Max.

"Although they didn't exactly have all the information," said Lucy.

Joe sighed. "I guess it's my fault," he said. "I told everyone that my nan would be here to look after us."

"So, who *is* here to look after you?" asked the inspector, raising an eyebrow.

Joe opened his mouth to reply and then stopped. He cocked his head to one side. "Did anyone else hear that?"

They all listened. From outside the castle came the distinctive sound of a car rolling up the gravel drive. The inspector checked her watch and frowned. "Who can that be? It's four in the morning. I thought the rest of my team had gone home."

Curious about who could be arriving so early, they all headed up the spiral staircase to the Great Hall. Joe opened the front door just as a big blue car pulled to a halt at the bottom of the steps. The car door opened and a large man got out and stretched, the way people do after a long drive.

"It's Dad!" cried Joe suddenly. "I'd forgotten that Mom said he'd be here by morning." He charged down the steps and threw his arms around his dad. He had been terrified of what his father would say when he arrived home all the way from Italy. But, after everything that had happened in the last few hours, Joe was overjoyed to see him.

Mike Carter was clearly taken by surprise. "Joe?" he said. "What on earth are you doing up at this time in the morning? And why is there a police car parked in the driveway?" He caught sight of the others gathered at the door and noticed the inspector and Miss Pollock. "And who are *those* people?"

Joe looked at his dad and couldn't stop grinning. "You'd better come inside, Dad," he said. "This is going to take quite a bit of explaining. You're never going to *believe* what's happened."

19

THE LAST WARRIOR

The inspector left shortly after Joe's dad arrived, saying she would contact them all in a day or two to let them know how the investigation was proceeding. After that, Mike Carter insisted on a full explanation before he would allow anyone to even think about going to bed.

It took a long time to tell the tale again and, even though it was extremely late, they thoroughly enjoyed having someone new to tell it to. Max and Joe in particular made such a good job of dramatizing their parts in the adventure that, by the end of the story, Mike Carter had turned quite pale. He sat back in an armchair in the Great Hall and mopped his forehead with the silk handkerchief from his blazer pocket.

"I can't believe four kids and a dog managed to create so much mayhem in just two days," he said. "The inspector said she thought that the newspapers would want to talk to you when they found out about it."

Joe grinned hopefully at his dad. "So, I guess you must be pretty proud of me then, Dad?"

His dad's eyebrows came together in a thick line across his forehead. "It's not quite as simple as that, young man." Joe's heart sank. "When your mother found out you'd come here without permission, she was beside herself with worry. You lied to us again, Joe, and nobody likes a liar."

In the silence that followed, Joe looked crestfallen. He dug his hands into his pants pockets and looked down at his shoes.

Then Max stepped forward and stood next to Joe. "Well, we like him," Max said. "I mean, I know he lied about his nan being here and everything, but he only did it because he wanted to give his friends a good time."

"And we did have a good time," said Charlie, coming to stand on the other side of Joe. "I'd never have gotten to stay in a place like this if it wasn't for him. The wildlife I've seen has been incredible."

"And don't forget that Joe was the one who rescued us," added Max. "If he hadn't found that secret entrance in the burial chamber, we might still be down there."

Then Lucy stepped forward so that they all stood shoulder to shoulder. "We know Joe shouldn't have lied to you, Mr. Carter," she said. "But we did have a terrific time while we were here. We're just sorry that we took you away from your vacation in Italy, that's all."

Mike Carter gave a snort and rolled his eyes. "A vacation in Italy? Don't make me laugh. You have no idea what it was like with those dreadful people. From morning to evening all they talked about were the latest fabrics, the length of their hemlines, and which handbag went best with their flip-flops. I thought I'd die of boredom."

Joe brightened. "So, does that mean you're not totally mad at me for having to come back?"

"Nice try, young man," said his father. "But as soon as I've had a short nap, I'm taking you all home to Southwold. With a bit of luck, I might even be able to get a round of golf in before I have to go back to work."

"Oh, so you're a golfer are you, Mr. Carter?" said Miss Pollock. She was coming up the stairs from the kitchen holding a tray, laden with mugs of hot tea. "Sorry, I couldn't help overhearing. I'm quite a keen player myself. There's a championship golf course quite near here. It's very exclusive but, if you were willing to stay a couple more days, you could come along as my guest." She glanced over at the children and gave them a broad wink.

Mike Carter blinked. "A championship golf course?" he repeated. "Near here?" He looked thoughtful. "I don't know..."

Joe grinned. "Go on, Dad. You're always saying how you never get enough time to play golf. You could stay here and play a few rounds and we could still be back in Southwold before Mom gets home." He tapped the side of his nose. "She never needs to know anything about it."

Mike Carter looked like a man who had just been offered a very large bribe. He looked at Joe, and then at Miss Pollock and then back at Joe again. Then he let out a huge sigh. "Oh, I just know I'm going to regret this," he said.

A short while later, the door to the castle roof burst open and four children and a small dog squeezed out through the narrow door. "Whose great idea was this?" complained Max, pulling his jacket tight. "I haven't slept for nearly twenty-four hours. All I want is my bed."

"Stop complaining," said Joe. "I just thought it would be nice to come up here and see the sunrise before we all go to sleep. Look at that view."

They gathered at the battlements and looked out across the field in the direction of the burial mound. The sky had already begun to brighten in the east and a thin line of red and gold was visible across the horizon.

"It's so beautiful here," said Lucy. "I can't believe you managed to persuade your dad to let us all stay until the weekend."

Joe grinned. "I think we've got Miss Pollock to

thank for that. Whoever knew she was such a good sport?"

"That means we can go to the lake again," said Charlie. "I might see those woodpeckers. And we can take Sherlock for long walks too."

At the mention of the word "walk," Sherlock looked up at his mistress, wagged his tale, and *ruff*ed. After a night of running through tunnels and barking at strangers, Sherlock was feeling

quite tired and his little legs ached. But, if his mistress still had enough energy for a walk, then Sherlock was determined that he was going with her.

"We can go swimming, every day," said Lucy.

"And there's still time to have another adventure before the weekend," said Joe.

"Oh, no," said Max, throwing up his hands. "No more adventures this week, please. You weren't the one who had to spend half the night in a haunted burial chamber."

"Haunted?" said Joe. "I thought you didn't believe in ghosts."

"I didn't," said Max. "I mean, I don't believe in ghosts exactly. But you've got to admit this place has..."

"An aura?" said Charlie.

Max smiled. "Yeah, something like that," he said.

Lucy squeezed Max's arm affectionately. "Well, don't worry," she said. "You won't have time for ghosts or adventures or anything else this week.

By my calculations, you still owe me two days' worth of math homework."

Max's eyes grew wide. "What? Lucy, you cannot be serious. Math homework? After everything we've been through?"

Lucy laughed.

"Look, the sun's coming up," said Joe.

Across the field, right behind the burial mound, the sun had appeared over the horizon like a great burnished shield, casting long shadows across the grass.

"It's beautiful," said Lucy. "I don't think I've ever stayed up all night to see the sunrise before."

They gazed at it for a long minute before Joe spoke again. "How about a snack before we all go to bed? We've got bacon and eggs, and there's still some sausages left from earlier."

Before anyone else could answer, Sherlock raised his head and barked, because "sausages" was one of the words that he understood very well. They all laughed and then began to file through the little door to head back to the kitchen.

Max was the last to leave the rooftop. He hung back after the others had gone and gazed across the field that was now bathed in the golden light of the sunrise. He'd had a glorious time with his friends and it wasn't over yet. He was sure that as long as he lived, he would never forget the mystery of Ufford Castle and the time they had discovered Ragnar's Gold.

As he turned to go, he spotted something strange in the glare of the sunrise. He looked again, then took off his glasses and cleaned them on his shirt before putting them back on. Then he frowned. There was nothing unusual there, he told himself, nothing at all.

But, just for a moment, when he had looked at the old burial mound, he could have sworn he had seen someone standing on the very top. A man, dressed in armor, carrying a round shield and a spear.

He blinked in surprise and swallowed. Then

he shook his head and smiled to himself before turning and going inside to eat bacon and eggs with his friends.

Author Note

The county of Suffolk in England is home to many mysteries, ghosts and ancient legends that made it the perfect inspiration for the After-School Detective Club.

For example, you may be interested to know that Black Shuck is a real local legend in Suffolk – a ghostly black dog, said to roam the countryside of East Anglia. According to those who have seen him, he is fierce and terrifying and prowls dark lanes and lonesome footpaths where his howling 'makes the blood run cold'.

Ufford Castle is based on Orford Castle which stands in the pretty town of Orford on the coast, and which boasts a maze of spooky passages, a basement, a chapel and real turrets. You can visit all year round, though there are no guarantees you will find any treasure!

Ragnar Lothbrok was a real Viking hero who carried out many fierce raids along the British coastline and plundered much treasure during the reign of the Anglo-Saxon king, Edmund the Martyr (who really did become king at the age of 14).

And lastly, Ragnar's gold itself was inspired by the fabulous Anglo-Saxon treasures found at Sutton Hoo, just a few miles down the road from Orford. The treasures included a golden helmet, weapons and countless pieces of jewellery found in the tomb of King Redwald and which can now be seen in the British Museum.

We really hope you enjoyed *The Secret of Ragnar's Gold* as much as we enjoyed researching and writing it and we look forward to seeing you again soon for the next adventure in the series.

Mark Dawson and Allan Boroughs

The After-School Detective Club are back in

The Mystery in the Marshes

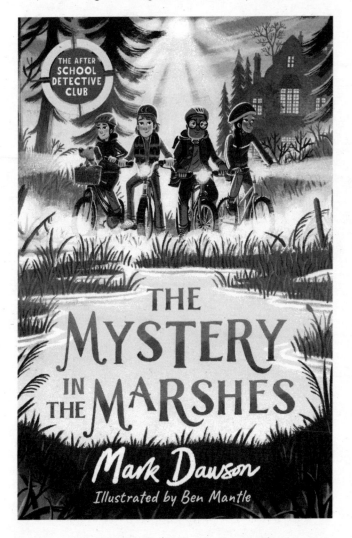

Read on for a preview of the opening chapter . . .

1

THE LETTER

Max Green stared in disbelief at the letter in his hands. He took a deep breath and forced himself to read the words again, his fingers trembling as their full meaning sank in.

'*Dear Maximillian,*' began the letter.

That was bad news for a start, thought Max. The only people who ever called him 'Maximillian' were his teachers and his mother, and it was rarely a good sign when they did.

'*This year, St Enid's School is participating in the prestigious 'Duke of Wellington' challenge, which encourages young people to develop the essential skills they need to survive in the wilderness.*

As one of our most academically gifted students, you are among those selected for the honour of participating in this rigorous outdoor assessment.'

Max closed his eyes and shuddered. The words 'rigorous' and 'outdoor assessment' really had no business being in a letter addressed to him. He continued reading.

'This year's challenge will take place in the beautiful Snape Marshes and the surrounding forests. All participants are expected to navigate their way on foot or by bicycle, spending no less than three nights under canvas and arriving at the final checkpoint by noon on the fourth day. You will be assessed on how well you perform your tasks with extra points awarded for demonstrating your survival skills and showing courage in the face of hardship. I do not need to tell you how important it is that our school does well in this exercise. _I know that you will not let the school down._'

The last line was underlined in red ink and the

letter was signed by the headteacher. Max gulped and looked up. On the other side of the breakfast table, his father was looking at him eagerly.

'Well?' said his dad when Max had finished reading. 'What do you think? Isn't it wonderful?'

'Wonderful?' echoed Max. 'They're going to make me live out of doors for four days in the cold and the wet, *under canvas!* That means living in an actual tent, Dad. It's like something out of the stone age. How is that wonderful exactly?'

Tony Green sighed. 'Now, don't be like that, Max,' he said, trying to keep the disappointment out of his voice and not entirely succeeding. 'When I was a boy, my friends and I were always off camping together in the summer months. It's the most fun a boy can have.'

Max put down the letter and held his head in his hands. 'The most fun a boy can have, Dad,' he said patiently, 'is spending the weekend in his bedroom with the new '*Warlocks and Dragons*' game, not sleeping in a field with a bunch of cows.

Why have they picked me to go on this thing anyway?'

'It's like the headmaster said in his letter,' said his mother as she placed a plateful of toast on the kitchen table. 'They picked you because you are one of their best students.'

'Yeah. They picked you because you're such a geek!' The small girl sitting at the end of the table grinned gleefully at Max, showing off the gap in her front teeth.

'That is enough from you, Safiyah,' said their mother raising a warning finger. 'Get on with your breakfast and don't annoy your brother.'

Max glared at his little sister. Even though she was only seven, Saffy always managed to be more irritating than a wasp at a picnic. When her mom wasn't looking, the little girl stuck her tongue out at Max before shovelling a spoonful of Frosty-Sparkles into her mouth and crunching noisily.

Max gave her a glare and turned back to his parents. 'Well, I can't go,' he said, breezily. 'I mean

I know it's a great honour and everything. But there's a competition at the chess club on Saturday and I simply have to be there."

'The competition can wait, Maximillian,' said his mother. 'Going on this adventure will be good for you and it will give you extra credit with the school which means you'll get even better grades next year. Besides, I've already signed the papers to say you have permission to go, so we'll hear no more about it.'

'You've signed the papers?' Max slumped in his chair with the air of a condemned man. 'So, I really can't get out of it?'

'Cheer up, Max,' said his dad. 'This trip will make a man of you.'

'Yeah,' said Max. 'That's just what I'm afraid of.'